Beloved in His Eyes

D1616885

Laurel O'Donnell

My Dear Reader -

Welcome to Beloved in His Eyes!

This is the story of Gawyn, Damien's brother from Angel's Assassin. While it isn't necessary to read Angel's Assassin or Cherished Protector of Her Heart first, you should definitely read them.

Gawyn has gone through his own challenges and obstacles in Angel's Assassin, but at the start of Beloved in His Eyes, he is settled and living with his brother. The stories take place in the fictional city of Acquitaine. While there is a real Aquitaine that is situated in France, the city where Gawyn lives lies somewhere in England.

Without further ado, I bring you Beloved in His Eyes!

Welcome to my world!

　　　-Laurel

Laurel O'Donnell

CHAPTER 1

Gawyn leaned against the stone wall, his arms crossed over his chest. He couldn't keep the grin from his lips as he watched his brother pace before the chair where Aurora, the lady of Acquitaine, his brother's wife, sat. It amused him to see Damien fight such a losing battle.

Damien was tall and imposing. He had an intense aura that frightened most people. Everyone, except Aurora. His brows furrowed in concern and determination, his jaw clenched. He shook his dark head. "I don't think you should go into town. Not today. The Hungars are angry with your decision to impose sanctions on trade with them."

Aurora watched him calmly. She allowed him to voice his concern patiently. She was beautiful, her long blonde hair immaculately braided behind her back, her small form just curvy enough to attract the attention of every man. She leaned forward, her small hands clenched before her as if in prayer. "Then they should not have imposed ridiculous road taxes on the merchants."

Damien paused before her. "I don't care about taxes or sanctions. I care about your safety."

She grinned at him, her blue eyes sparkling.

Gawyn shook his head slightly. Damien was doomed to lose this argument. He would never convince Aurora not to go into town to visit her people. But he also knew that Damien was right. It was dangerous.

"I know. And I know you will do everything in your power to keep me safe," Aurora said gently.

Damien clenched his teeth and closed his eyes.

Aurora stood and moved to him. She placed her hands on his shoulders. "I have to go in to town."

"Just to visit your people. Your safety should be more important."

She ran her fingers along Damien's cheek. "If I don't, it will tell the Hungars that I am frightened by their threats. It will be admitting that I am afraid. My people, all of Acquitaine, all of the Hungars, must know that I am not afraid."

Gawyn had to admire her. She was a great ruler. She protected her people. Her city flourished. And she was smart. A kind and wise ruler. In this instance, he agreed with her. She could not show fear to the barbarians that neighbored Acquitaine.

Damien inhaled slowly. He nodded his head once, in agreement.

Aurora leaned forward and pressed her lips to his in a long kiss. Then, she leaned her forehead against his. "I am sorry to have to make your job more difficult."

Damien shook his head again, his dark hair swaying slightly above his shoulders. "I would do anything for you," he whispered. "Except lose you. I can't do that."

Aurora hugged him fiercely. "You won't ever have to do that."

Damien lowered his lips to claim hers, his arms wrapped around her small frame to pull her close.

Gawyn looked away. He knew how much they loved each other. He knew Damien would do everything he could to keep Aurora safe. Yet, he had known the outcome of this argument before Damien had spoken a word of objection.

When they separated, Aurora stepped back from Damien. "And, don't forget, my cousin, Megan will be arriving in two days."

Damien kissed her hand before releasing it. "I remember."

Aurora moved to the door and exited. Damien followed. He paused long enough to grumble to Gawyn, "Double the guard."

Gawyn smiled. "I already have."

Damien tore his gaze from Aurora to glance at Gawyn. "You think this is funny?"

"Only because it's you, brother.

Damien huffed. "One day, you'll find your own wife. And I'll be one the laughing." He moved out of the judgement room.

Gawyn watched after his brother. Aurora had saved Damien in so many ways. He was a different man, now. As Gawyn was. Gawyn knew that Aurora had saved them both. He would be lucky to find a woman like her. Until then, his job was to see her safe, and to remain loyally at his brother's side.

"Are you sure she comes this way?" the boy asked in excitement, straining on his toes to see above the head of the two men in front of them, toward the dirt street.

Justina Auber looked down at her younger brother, Adam. At a mere ten summers, he was thin and wiry, but very energetic. He hopped up and down. His dirty blonde hair was tangled and unkempt and he swiped it from his eyes. She grinned at his excitement. He had worked hard for a month at home, on her uncle's farm, to get this opportunity. Yet, Justina couldn't believe he was this excited. He had spoken of nothing else since she and her uncle told him they would be going into town to see Lady Aurora. Justina began calling her Adam's princess. She shrugged slightly. "That's what uncle said." And by the looks of the gathering crowd, he had been told correctly.

They stood near a baker's shop, purchasing a loaf of bread. When they had first arrived, the gathered villagers moved effortlessly through the square. Now, it was growing crowded with merchants, villagers, and visitors.

Justina and Adam lived outside of Acquitaine and had made the day long track into the city just to get a glimpse of Lady Aurora. Ever since Adam overheard a knight speak of her beauty and her kindness, he couldn't stop talking about her.

Adam grabbed Justina's hand. "Come on! We must get to the street. We'll miss her!"

Justina almost dropped the loaf of bread as Adam jerked her arm. She righted the loaf, but lost hold of his hand. She hurried behind him. She saw his bobbing head disappear between a farmer and a merchant. "Adam!"

"Sweet cider!" someone called from a building behind her.

Justina searched desperately for a resurgence of Adam's head in the sea of people lining the road. She was not considered short, but even at eighteen summers, she had to stand on her toes to see around and over the tops of some of the heads. Someone bumped her, and she juggled the loaf for a moment. "Adam!"

Adam appeared before her, seized her hand, and began to pull her into the crowd of villagers and merchants. "Hurry! We're going to miss her!"

The market square was so crowded, they could barely squeeze around villagers. Merchants shouted from shop windows, hawking their wares. "Venison! Get your venison!"

A farmer Justina passed reeked of sweet hay. Somewhere behind them a dog barked. The world seemed to swirl as Adam pulled her through the crowd of people.

Adam paused for a moment and Justina turned to look up at the shop window where a fat merchant sat, calling out. Adam jerked her forward and she slammed into a man's back. He whirled on her, glaring hotly. She mumbled an apology and called out to Adam.

She remembered one other town where it had been this crowded. A tightness began in her chest, but she quickly pushed the memory aside. It wasn't a good memory and she had no desire to see it again now. Still, the haunting similarity shook her. Unease spread through her and then Adam jerked her forward. She instinctively followed him. The panic lingered as she curved and dodged around all sorts of people. Some merchants, some farmers, some knights. Some dressed as she and Adam were, in plain colors, others wore vibrant hues. Faces blurred past her. There were so many. Voices rose around her, some loud and gruff, some quiet and timid. "Adam!" she called. Her brother would not slow down. He was determined to be in the front. She skirted a rather large man wearing a ripped tunic.

Adam paused and released her wrist as silence spread over the square like a warm breeze. It was almost magical, the way it moved over the crowd and, as one, the sea of people turned toward the road. Tingles raced along the nape of Justina's neck. She craned her neck in an attempt to see over the taller men in front of her. She couldn't see what was happening.

And then, Adam was moving again. She followed him through the maze of legs, ducking and squirming between them. It was hot and muggy in the midst of all these people, but Justina somehow managed to follow her brother. Suddenly, he was gone. She paused looking for his dirty blonde hair and tan tunic. Panic gripped her. She searched down low, through the legs of the bystanders. When there was no sight of him, she rose and stood on the tips of her toes, desperately trying to find him. She whirled, searching, but there was no sign of him. He had to have moved forward to see his princess. She shoved forward, toward the street and burst out of the crowd into the road.

Fresh air assailed her as she spun to look for her brother. Instead, her eyes locked on a man. Black eyes, black clothing, black hair. She froze. Dread and fear gripped her in an icy hand. She couldn't move. She recognized him immediately. The monster who had killed her father. He was descending on her like the grim reaper. She shrunk away, recognizing those dark eyes, that face. She could never forget him. Her breath left her. He grabbed her arm. A terrified noise issued from her throat.

"Damien."

The monster looked over his shoulder toward the voice.

An angel appeared, her pale face and white dress almost glowing in the bright sunlight. She lay her hand on the monster's arm. "You're scaring her."

The monster turned his dead, cold gaze to Justina and her world spun. For a moment, she thought he was going to kill her. That face. She would never forget that face.

"Justina!" Adam's voice rang out.

Horrified the monster would turn his attention to her brother, she struggled in his hold. She stared at Adam who was approaching her with a skip in his step and joy in his brown eyes. She held a hand out to stop him. But he came closer, a grin on his lips. Her heart pounded, and she looked back at the monster. He pulled her closer.

This was the end. He was going to kill her. She held up her hands to prevent the deadly strike.

"Watch where you're going," he snarled. Then, he released her arm. She tumbled to the ground on her backside, smashing the loaf of bread in the dust of the road. The monster turned away.

Cold engulfed her and she shivered. A jumble of emotions tumbled inside of her. Relief, fear. Paralyzed, she watched him leave her, watched him walk away. Tears rose in her eyes, stinging and burning. It took a moment for her to realize he wasn't going to kill her. Free of his numbing hold, anger flared to life, extinguishing all her rational feelings. Like a silent accusation, she felt the cool metal of the dagger she always wore strapped to her thigh. Why hadn't she used it? She had been too afraid. And that made her even more angry. How many times had she vowed to kill the monster? How many times had she imagined coming face to face with him and plunging the dagger into his chest? "I know you," she whispered. Even her words came out shaky.

But it was enough. He stopped, his shoulders straightening before he slowly turned to her. Their gazes locked. That black, evil gaze pinned her to the spot.

She lifted her chin and narrowed her eyes. Come back, she silently begged and reached toward her leg. I won't miss my chance again.

But the monster turned and continued walking away.

"Did you see her?"

She was trembling fiercely. He wasn't coming back! She had missed her opportunity! Grimacing, she pushed herself to her feet, half drawing the dagger from the sheath at her thigh.

"Justina. Did you see her?"

Slowly, everything around her came back into focus. The murmuring of the crowd. The shout of the guard to "stand aside". Adam beside her, shaking her arm. Still, she watched the monster move. Such power, strength in every step.

"She was right next to you!" Adam groaned. "I should have stayed with you."

Adam. Justina released the handle of the dagger. It wasn't worth losing her brother.

The monster paused beside another man. A man the same size as he with brown hair. The two spoke. And then, slowly, they both turned to her. The second man nodded. His eyes lit on her with acuteness.

Justina rose, seizing Adam's arm. They had to get out of there. She pulled him back into the crowd, hoping to disappear amongst the throngs of villagers and merchants. She moved quickly, hauling Adam behind her, holding his arm in a tight grip.

"What?" he hollered. The farther away from the

road they moved, the louder the environment became. Merchants shouted about long burning candles, one merchant promised to grant youth with his concoction.

As they neared the candle maker's shop, Adam broke free from her hold. "What did I do? Why are we leaving?"

Justina scanned the crowd for the monster or his friend. She knew they would be coming for her. Why couldn't she have just kept her mouth closed? "It's time to leave."

"Why? We've got the entire day!"

Justina glanced at Adam. "You've seen your princess. It's time to go home."

"I don't want to go back yet."

"Adam," she said sternly, grabbing his arms, and shaking him slightly. "I promised you'd get to see your princess. You have. We have to leave." She took his hand into hers and whirled, leading him toward the road.

They hurried in silence for a moment, until Adam asked, "What happened?"

Justina's hand tightened around Adam's instinctively, protectively. She had endangered his life. Lord, if anything happened to her brother. If anything... She couldn't tell him. He could never know how their father had died. Ignorance might save his life. "I almost ran into your princess. They might want to throw me in the dungeon."

"Nay," Adam insisted, turning to look over his shoulder. "They would never throw you in the dungeon. Lady Aurora would understand."

Justina didn't stop. "You can say that. But she is a lady and I almost crashed into her. We must hurry before the guards come."

Adam was silent.

Justina thought the issue was over. She thought

Adam would understand the offense she was fleeing from. Yet, it was a much bigger issue she faced than almost crashing into a lady. That monster. She recognized him. She was certain he would not risk her telling others what he had done, what kind of person he was. He couldn't let her live, she was certain.

CHAPTER 2

Gawyn hunched beneath a bush, watching the small, dark farmhouse.

It was easy to fall back into the training he had received as an assassin, even though he had lived with Damien and Aurora in Acquitaine now for almost a year. He had tracked the young woman and boy back to a farm on the outskirts of Auch. It had taken a day travel on foot. They had barely rested. Almost as if they were running away from something.

In the square at Acquitaine, Gawyn had seen the fear in the girl's wide eyes as she stared at his brother. Did she know Damien had been an assassin? That couldn't be allowed. For a moment, he thought of his options. Dungeon, stocks. Gawyn stopped himself. She was a slip of a girl. What danger could she possibly pose to the Lord of Acquitaine? Still, he knew it only took one person to destroy a man, be he King or peasant. He didn't know who the boy and girl were. Or how the girl knew Damien. He would find out how she knew his brother and discuss the matter with him.

He was grateful that he had options. He thought back

to a time when his only recourse would be slitting her throat, a time when killing had been the only answer. Now, things were different. Now, *he* was different. He lived among civilized people. He didn't think like that anymore.

He heard the crunch of a twig behind him and froze. Prickles raced along his spine. He reached for his sword and whirled...

...only to find the tip of a dagger blade pointed at him.

A tiny blade. He almost laughed aloud. The small blade might give him a little wound, but certainly wouldn't kill him. His gaze moved from the point of the dagger to the holder. The girl, the one he had been following.

A grin quirked his lips. She had snuck up on him! It looked like his training wasn't as sharp as it used to be. Either that or the girl was incredibly good at sneaking up on someone. Gawyn's gaze swept her. She was just the slip of a girl, her body was hidden beneath a cotton cloak. Dappled moonlight fell onto riotous brown hair that hung in curls about her shoulders. Her eyes were narrowed, her lips set in a thin, determined line. She held the blade out before her steadily, unflinchingly.

He removed his hand from his sword's hilt and lifted them, so she could see both hands. He was certain that even if she stabbed him, he wouldn't die.

She jutted the dagger toward him. "What are you doing here?"

He backed up a step. "Careful. I was trying to find you."

"I know you."

All humor left him. Had she recognized him, as well as Damien? In his other life, working for Roke, he had killed many people. An assassin with a flair for poison. But that was over a year ago, another lifetime ago. He didn't move, but all his senses heightened, ready. Ready for what? He had no intention of killing her.

"You were with the other man at the castle with the princess."

He scowled, confused. Other man? Damien? Princess? Well, that had to be Aurora. No one else fit that description. He opened his mouth to question her, but she was quicker.

"Why were you trying to find me? What do you want?" Her hand tightened around the handle of the blade.

"I came..." She jabbed the blade at him and he stepped back. "Whoa. Watch that."

Her hand shook, and the blade wobbled slightly.

She wasn't as sure of herself as Gawyn first thought. He didn't want to scare her or upset her.

"You followed me," she accused.

Gawyn was sure he could disarm her easily enough. But not yet. "I had to. How else was I going to invite you to dine at the castle?"

Her mouth dropped slightly. The dagger lowered a fraction. "Dine at the castle?" she repeated.

"You and your brother."

Her eyes narrowed suspiciously, sparkling in the muted moonlight. "Sneaking around in the middle of the night to invite me to the castle?" Her voice was full of suspicion.

He liked the way the moonlight caught in her eyes. "I wasn't sneaking. I couldn't very well knock on your door at this time of night." He smiled his most dashing grin and reached out. "Now, let's have that weapon –"

She grabbed his arm and flipped him over her leg.

13

He landed on his back in the dirt, the tip of her blade pressed to his throat.

"What do you want? Who are you?"

Shock gave way to admiration. He was beginning to really like her. No one had landed him on his back, ever. She was full of surprises. "My name is Gawyn. I am captain of the guard at Castle Acquitaine."

"Why would we be invited to dine at the castle? We're just farmers."

"I don't question Lord Damien. He said for me to find you and invite you to dine at the castle." At least the first part was true, he did want him to find her.

"Lord Damien?" She scowled. "He doesn't even know who we are. I want you off my lands."

"It's very disrespectful to deny an invitation from your lord."

"*My* lord?" she repeated straightening.

Gawyn slowly climbed to his feet. "You are a tenant on Acquitaine lands. You pay a yearly tithe."

She harrumphed and lowered the blade. "Unfortunately, *my* lord doesn't know we exist. We are so far removed from the city that we mean nothing to him. Where was he when the Hungars raided the farm next to us? Where was he when disease ravished our livestock and we went hungry for most of the year?"

Gawyn dusted the dirt and debris from his leggings. "Did you present these issues to Lady Aurora?"

She chuckled without humor. "It's a day's walk to get to the city. One way. I can't afford to be away from the farm for two days."

"Yet, you were there today."

Those expressive eyes narrowed again. Her gaze

moved quickly over him, and she took a step away. "And I have to make up the chores I missed by being there. So, I must decline the invitation to dine at the castle. With all due respect."

"I shall give Lord Damien your regrets." He judged her with an appreciative summative glance. Just a young woman. Surely, she was no threat to Damien. "May I have your name?"

She placed her free hand on her hip. "Lord Damien requested my presence to dine at the castle without knowing my name?" she asked in disbelief.

Gawyn shrugged. "He can't possibly know every person who resides on his lands."

"Obviously." She leaned back against a tree, watching him. She twirled the dagger handle in her fingers. "If he wants to know my name, he can ask me himself."

Gawyn smiled outright. She was feisty. He really liked her. He bowed slightly. "I shall relay your message."

"When you leave, stay to the left of the road. There has been reports of bandits to the east."

Oh, she was intriguing! It had been a long time since he had found a woman who could match wits with him. He nodded and turned to go but paused. He reached into his jupon and turned back to her, holding a loaf of bread out.

Her eyes shifted to the bread.

"You dropped a loaf in the street. I'd hate for you to return from Acquitaine empty handed."

She narrowed her eyes suspiciously but snatched the bread from his hand. A grin started on his lips, but he hid it by turning away.

CHAPTER 3

Exhausted, Gawyn, heading for his chambers, entered Castle Acquitaine. He had ridden all night and planned to sleep after he told Damien the farm girl was no threat. He had been unable to stop thinking about the young woman for the entire ride home. She was an enigma for a farm girl. Where had she learned to defend herself like that? Of course, he would never tell Damien that she had managed to land him on his back.

He skirted servants rushing down the corridor, hurrying to prepare for the day. He took the spiral stairway two at a time. He was not surprised to see Aurora and Damien at the top of the stairs. Aurora rose early, like the sun, Damien with her.

"Good morn, Gawyn," Aurora greeted cheerfully. She scowled, her gaze perusing his face. "You have not been to bed, have you?"

Gawyn glanced at Damien and then back to Aurora. "Not yet. I had a pressing matter to attend to." He glanced quickly at Damien.

"Is it taken care of?" Damien asked.

"There is nothing to take care of. There is no threat."

Damien nodded. "Thank you, brother." He put a hand on Aurora's back to steer her toward the stairs.

Gawyn stepped before them. "There is no immediate threat, but I was informed that an Auch farm had been raided by the Hungars."

Aurora turned to him in surprise. "Why were we not notified of this?"

Damien stepped toward him, a scowl marring his brow. "When?"

Gawyn looked at Aurora. "It takes a day's walk to get to Acquitaine from Auch. Many of the farmers don't have steeds to ride. A day's trip deprives them of priceless time away from their crops and animals."

Aurora glanced at Damien. "Don't we have sentries or men there to protect them?"

"They were attacked recently. The other day, I believe," Gawyn answered Damien. "Auch needs reinforcements."

"Take a squadron and set up a perimeter. I don't want the Hungars on Acquitaine lands."

Aurora nodded in agreement.

As Gawyn moved to pass them, she lay a gentle hand on his arm.

"But first, get some rest."

Justina rose at dawn. She still didn't like the idea of some man lurking in the forest, especially if he was the captain of the guard. All she needed was him to be killed by bandits on the way home and a storm of Acquitaine guards would swarm down on the farm. Maybe his presence should have been reassuring to her, as protection from the Hungars. But he was only one man. A man whom she had seen speaking with a monster.

She winced. She never should have agreed to take Adam into town. How did the captain of the guard know that monster?

She took a bowl from the table and filled it with porridge from the brewing pot in the hearth. Then she sat at the table.

Adam strolled into the room, yawning, and stretching. He got a bowl, filled it with porridge and sat across from Justina. He took two sips before commenting, "You were up late."

Prickles raced along her spine. She tried to be casual. "I was checking on the pigs."

"No, you weren't. You didn't go to the sty. You circled around the other way."

She looked at him. "How do you know that?"

"I followed you."

She froze in dread. With that captain of the guard hiding in the brush, he could have been hurt! Damn. She took a sip from the porridge, trying to remain calm. "You shouldn't be out so late."

"Who was that man?"

He had seen him! She clenched her teeth and wiped her mouth with her sleeve to hide her uncertainty. She could lie to him, but she wasn't certain if he had heard their conversation. She sighed. "No one of import."

"He said he was the captain of the guard."

Justina put the bowl down. "Why did you ask if you already knew the answer?"

Adam sipped his porridge. He ran a sleeve across his mouth. "What did he want? Did he come to take you to the dungeon?"

"No. No. Nothing like that."

"Then what did he want? Why was he out there in the middle of the night? Why didn't he just come and talk to Uncle Bruce?"

Justina took a deep breath. "It's nothing for you to worry about. He won't be back." She sipped some porridge from her bowl.

"He's the captain of the guard! Are you in trouble for bumping into Lady Aurora? Are you going to be arrested?"

Justina shook her head. "Everything will be fine, Adam. Don't worry. Where is Uncle Bruce?"

"He is out with the geese and pigs." Adam sat back in his chair, his meal forgotten as his mind raced with horrible possibilities. "He found out where you live. They're going to come back and arrest you. You were right! We have to –"

"He's not going to arrest me."

"What else could it...?" He lifted his gaze to hers. His brown eyes were wide and alarmed. "You'll be thrown in the dungeon and then what shall I do?"

"Adam! I will not be thrown in the dungeon."

Adam scowled and stared at his porridge quietly for a moment, thinking. Then, his eyebrows shot up. He leaned forward in his chair. "Maybe Uncle Bruce can't pay the tithe. Maybe they won't come for you, but for him!"

"Adam!" Panic flared inside her. She reached across the table to grab Adam's arm. "You can't tell Uncle Bruce about this."

Adam's brow furrowed. "Why not?"

"I don't want Uncle Bruce to be alarmed. He has

enough on his mind. He doesn't need to know about this."

"If the captain of the guard came to arrest him –"

Justina knew Adam would keep asking about the captain of the guard, like a gnat festering a wound. She had no choice. "He didn't come to arrest anyone!"

"Maybe Uncle Bruce is in trouble. Maybe --"

She had to tell him. She sighed heavily. "He asked us to dine at the castle."

Silence. It was almost worse than the constant questions. Adam's eyes widened. Bigger. Brighter. Filled with excitement. "We're going to dine at the castle?"

"No."

"No?"

"I told him no."

His shoulders slouched in disappointment. "Why? Why would you do that?"

"Adam," Justina said quietly, with as much patience as she could muster. "We were gone for two days. We can't do that to Uncle Bruce again. It's too much work for him. He's getting old. He needs us." She sipped the porridge from her bowl again. "We had our time to visit the city and to see your princess. It was kind of Uncle Bruce to allow us to go. But it is our responsibility to help him."

"You didn't even ask him if it was okay."

"Adam, I said no. I don't want to leave Uncle Bruce alone. Not with the raids on the farms so close. I'm worried about the Hungars coming to harm him."

Adam sat back in his chair, crossing his arms over his chest. His lower lip pouted.

"I'm sorry, Adam. It's just not a good idea." She would never tell him the real reason she didn't want to go. Their father's killer was a friend of the captain of the guard.

She never wanted to see that monster again. And she never wanted Adam to be near him. Never.

Later that day, as the sun was coming down in the sky, Justina was working in the garden, picking the fresh peas and placing the pods in the basket.

A thundering noise started low from down the road and grew. She looked up. Over the trees a large cloud of dust rose. For a moment, she thought it was fire, but couldn't understand what the loud rumble was. She glanced back at the field where Adam was feeding the ox. He had stopped working and was turned in the direction of the road.

Uncle Bruce emerged from the house, a stalwart man, wearing a cotton brown tunic and breeches. His wheat hat waved in the breeze and he had to hold it on for a moment as he gazed down the road. He straightened and shouted, "Inside!" He raced back toward the cruck.

Justina dropped the basket and ran toward the house. Hungars. Chills peppered the nape of her neck as she raced toward the cruck. Could it be the Hungars raiding their farm? She met Adam halfway to the house and they exchanged concerned glances while running. Uncle Bruce raced toward them until he caught up. He took up a protective pace behind them, urging them forward with quick waves of his hands, and jogged behind them.

A large group of horses emerged on the road, thundering toward them. The lead one held a banner and on it was a white dove. The heraldry for Acquitaine. They slowed their run and when they realized there was no threat, turned in unison toward the group of mounted men. As the men closed the distance, Justina saw they wore tunics with the Acquitaine heraldry on them. Soldiers.

Uncle Bruce stepped before Justina and Adam to greet the men.

As they reined up before them, Justina's eyebrows rose in shock as she recognized the leader. The captain of the guard. What was his name? Gawyn.

He was an imposing figure atop the horse. Black boots were in the stirrups. He wore a chest plate of armor, but no other armor. His thick, shoulder-length brown hair waved in the breeze. He grinned at her, his brown eyes twinkling, before turning his resolute gaze to Uncle Bruce.

A strange flutter deep in Justina's chest responded to his perfect smile.

"We've received word that the Hungars have been raiding farms along the Acquitaine border." He glanced at Justina and then back at Bruce. "Has your farm been attacked?"

"No, Sir," Bruce stuttered. "But the farm east of us has had problems."

Gawyn signaled a man with a wave of his hand. The man rode up to him. Gawyn looked at Bruce. "The farmer's name?"

"Montague," Bruce answered.

"Take half the men and secure the Montague farm."

"Aye, Captain." The man signaled some men and they rode off down the road.

Gawyn swung his leg over the horse and dismounted. He stopped before Justina and nodded to her. "Good to see you again, Justina."

Shocked, Justina's mouth dropped open, too stunned to reply. How did he know her name?

He smiled at her. "Lady Aurora and Lord Damien send their regards." He leaned in close to her. "Sometimes it's worth it to take the two-day trip into the city."

Justina watched in startlement as he moved passed her to her uncle. He had listened to her!

"A word about your borders and your livestock," Gawyn said. Uncle Bruce nodded and led the way into the cruck, but not before he locked gazes with Justina. There was relief and happiness in his eyes.

For a long moment, Justina stood in shock. The captain of the guard, Gawyn, had brought soldiers to defend them. He had listened to what she said the night before! Warmth blossomed in her chest. She wasn't exactly sure what to make of him, whether to thank him or be distrustful of him.

Adam tugged on her arm. "Did you see his sword?"

She had seen his sword. But that wasn't what was intriguing her. It was his eyes, the merry way they gleamed at her. There was just something about him. She nodded. "I saw it."

Gawyn emerged from the cruck, Bruce following. He was a hard-working farmer who was trying to look out for his family, his animals and his crops. He had given his word to report back to the city. But Gawyn had other plans. He would not leave the farm unprotected. Not with the Hungars so close. His gaze swept the lands. An ox ate grass not far from the house, pigs roamed nearby, and the quacking of geese sounded in the distance. Healthy fields encircled the house. Most of them had been harvested. There were still peas left. His gaze halted on the field of peas where he noticed Justina working at harvesting them. She was bent over in a simple cotton dress; her dark hair fell in waves about her shoulders. She paused to brush a strand from her cheek before she continued. No one would ever know she was a force to be reckoned with. He wondered if Bruce knew.

Gawyn had been given specific orders to get her back to the city and to find out how she knew Damien. A mission he intended to accomplish. Shouldn't be hard. He moved toward her when a little whirlwind of a child stepped before him. The boy's dirty blonde hair was unkempt with a leaf sticking out of it near his ear.

Gawyn swore he saw the rest of the branch buried in his wild head of hair.

"Is it true?" the boy asked. "Are you the captain of the guard?"

"Aye," Gawyn answered. The boy circled him, inspecting every aspect.

"That's a big sword. Is your chest plate heavy?" Gawyn opened his mouth to answer, but the boy stepped before him again, looking up at him with wonder-filled eyes. "I would have liked to eat at the castle, but Justina said we couldn't make the trip."

"Your sister works hard."

The boy nodded. "So does Uncle Bruce. We all work from dawn til sunset. My favorite part is tending the ox. He's so big. Do you think he's bigger than your horse?"

Gawyn raised his eyebrow. He didn't need to answer the boy. The boy would just continue to ask questions. He was a curious child. In time, he would learn that to become wise, he needed answers.

"I once saw a horse that was twice the size of yours."

"Adam," Justina called as she approached. "Leave

24

Captain Gawyn alone. He has enough work to do without you bothering him."

Gawyn looked at the boy and made a mental note of his name. Adam. "It was probably a war horse. When you come to Castle Acquitaine, I'll show you my war horse."

"You have a war horse?" Adam gasped.

Gawyn nodded.

"Adam, I thought I saw a cat near the geese. Go chase it away," Justina ordered.

The boy's joyful expression faded, and anger danced in his eyes. He whirled, racing away toward the field, mumbling something about troublesome cats.

Justina watched him leave before turning back to Gawyn. "You shouldn't tell him things like that. We won't be going to Acquitaine any time soon. I told you the trip was too long. I can't be away from my chores."

Gawyn smiled. "I think you'll be there sooner than you think. Remember? Lord Damien requested your presence at dinner."

Justina scowled. "Is that why you brought all these soldiers?"

"I brought all these soldiers under Lady Aurora's orders. She is particularly protective of her people. She will see to it that your uncle is safe."

"You told her about us?"

"I told her about the Hungars raiding a farm. She was concerned about the people living on the borders. She really was hurt you could not travel and inform her of the danger. So..." He turned back toward the group of soldiers who had dismounted and were awaiting orders. He scanned the men until his gaze fell upon a white and brown horse near the front of the line. He pointed to it. "See that horse? The one with the brown markings?"

Justina nodded.

"Lady Aurora is giving her to you so that your trip will not take so long."

Justina gasped. She opened her mouth and then closed it, staring at the animal. Finally, she looked at Gawyn. "I... I... I don't know what to say."

Gawyn smiled, enjoying her speechlessness. "You can come to dinner and thank her."

CHAPTER 4

Just as Captain Gawyn had predicted, Uncle Bruce had insisted Justina and Adam return to Acquitaine and thank Lady Aurora. Justina knew that Uncle Bruce could use the extra horse on the farm. They were very thankful for Lady Aurora's help. And still, Justina was apprehensive about returning to Acquitaine.

Her father's murderer was in Acquitaine. What would she do if she came face to face with him? And what of Adam? Would he be safe?

Uncle Bruce had insisted, and Justina couldn't say no. Not only had Lady Aurora given them a horse, but she had stationed soldiers on the borders of the land. Since the soldiers were there, Justina knew Uncle Bruce was well protected. While there was still work to be done on the farm, she felt obligated to thank Lady Aurora. Since the harvest was mostly finished, this was an opportune time to go to the city. There was less work to do on the farm.

She had agreed to the trip.

She rode the new mare Lady Aurora had given them. She cast a glance at Adam who was delighted to ride with the captain. Justina wondered how long it would be until Gawyn couldn't take it anymore and made Adam ride with her. She looked down and smiled secretly. Served him right. He was so confident they would accept Lord Damien's request to dine with them.

He had been right. Still, Justina couldn't stop the apprehension that grew inside of her the closer they got to Acquitaine. She couldn't get the image of that face, those cold eyes, out of her mind. What could she do about her father's killer? What if she saw him again? She would plunge her dagger into his heart for killing her father! She would make sure she didn't miss her opportunity this time. As they moved, she placed her hand over the dagger strapped to her thigh. She had planned and visualized the moment for a long time. She knew what she had to do.

"I'm glad you changed your mind."

Startled, Justina lifted her gaze. Gawyn was riding next to her. Adam's eyes were on the two knights ahead of them. "About what?"

"Lord Damien's invitation."

"I'm glad, too," Adam said.

"I had little choice. I would have ended up in the dungeon if I didn't personally make the trip to thank Lady Aurora."

Gawyn grinned softly.

Justina gaped, realizing how her statement sounded. "I meant no offense to Lady Aurora! I meant Uncle Bruce would have –"

Gawyn shook his head. "You have nothing to apologize for. I took no offense and Lady Aurora would not have, either. She really cares for her people and was very upset she had not been informed of the raid."

Justina nodded. She felt a wave of embarrassment wash through her. "Thank you for relaying the message." Gawyn stared at her so intently that a blush rose in her cheeks.

"How could I do anything else?"

Justina lowered her gaze and suddenly found herself staring at Adam. His brow was furrowed in confusion as he stared at her. She quickly averted her gaze to the reins of the horse she held in her hand.

"How many guards are at the castle?" Adam asked.

Thank the Lord for Adam, Justina thought.

"Will I get to meet all of them?"

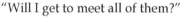

They made it to Acquitaine as the sun was beginning to set. The two soldiers rode in the front, Gawyn and Adam behind Justina. They emerged from the forest to a breathtaking sight. Justina couldn't help but gasp in awe. The setting sun bathed the wall of the city in a beautiful, multi-colored glow. Even though Justina had visited Acquitaine a few days ago, she would never get used to the grand sight.

A wide, green valley stretched before them with a road snaking through it. Like little ants, people walked down the dirt road away from the city. A moat surrounded the city and led to the river running beside it. A drawbridge extended over the moat and wagons, knights and people moved in and out of the large, welcoming wooden gates of the city.

Between the merlons of the city wall, Justin could make out the knights on patrol. Over the wall, she saw rows of thatched houses lining the streets. Acquitaine was a huge, bustling city. Shops, homes, and guilds all resided inside these walls. This was where the square was where Justina and Adam had first seen the Lady Aurora. Yes, it was exciting, but it held darker things. The city was where Justina saw the monster who had killed her father.

Inside the city, near the river, was the grandest castle Justina had ever seen, not that she had seen many, but this one was beautiful. Another moat surrounded the castle, wider than the one around the city. Another higher stone wall surrounded the castle.

Beyond the inner wall was the castle itself. Above the wall, Castle Acquitaine rose like a sleeping giant, monumental and shining in the bright sunlight. Towers of stone rose to the sky and tiny flags flapped in the wind on top of the stone turrets. Four tall, elegant towers rose into the sky, bordered by merlons. One tower was taller than the rest in the back near the river. Justina remembered hearing that this was where Lady Aurora's father had leapt from and died. She remembered how sad she had been for Lady Aurora.

The gate to the castle was open, the drawbridge extending across the moat.

Gawyn started forward, moving down the road toward the gates to the village. As they neared the walls, Adam turned his head from one side to the other, taking everything in. He pointed at a colorful wagon before them, then his finger shifted to a knight on horseback galloping from the city.

The knight nodded at Gawyn.

They passed through the large wooden gates into the city. The roads were crowded with people, all heading out of the city. Justina turned to look at the setting sun. It was getting late and she knew the people were heading to their homes. Some would remain in the city, but most had homes outside the gates.

Around them, shop keepers called out their wares to the passing crowd. "Don't forget your warm blanket! Perfect for a cold night!" "Don't leave without trying Tom's sweet ale!"

Justina lifted her gaze to the castle before them. It was huge. Castle Acquitaine soared in the distance like a grand mountain. Square towers loomed into the sky on each end of the castle. She twisted to look behind her. Guards walked the battlements at the top of the city walls. The line of people leaving the city seemed unending. She turned forward again. Two days ago, when she and Adam had come into the city, it was to catch a glimpse of his princess. She had been in charge. She knew when they were leaving, how they would go. Now, unease gripped her. She didn't know what to expect. Her gaze moved up the towering castle to the sky above. She felt insignificant.

Justina dropped her gaze from the soaring towers of the castle to the dusty street. She met the questioning gaze of a woman carrying an empty basket and quickly looked away. How was she different from the woman? How had she ended up catching the eye of the captain of the guard?

The crowds on the roads parted for the line of horses as they marched through city. She swiveled her gaze to the lead horse. Gawyn cantered his animal down the street with confidence. A sense of calm came over her as she watched him handle his horse, his stare on the road ahead. His back was straight despite the heavy plate mail on his chest. He wore no helmet like the rest of the soldiers; instead he let his brown hair flow free in the breeze. She liked it much better and found herself grinning as she watched him.

They moved across the drawbridge of the castle and

beneath the raised portcullis. Justina looked up at the spikes on the end of the portcullis as they passed beneath the heavy metal gate. She would hate to have it slam shut on her head and cringed slightly. It was massive.

They continued into the outer ward and then the inner ward where they came to a halt. The two soldiers dismounted, and young boys rushed to take the reins of their horses. Justina shifted in the saddle, looking this way and that. That same unease came back, spreading through her body. What about her horse? Should she just leave it? She was unaccustomed to this luxury.

And then Gawyn stood beside her. He reached up for her, putting his hands around her waist, and eased her from her horse. Warmth blossomed across her cheeks as her toes touched the ground and she found her hands on his strong shoulders. For a moment, she could say nothing, do nothing, but stare into his deep brown eyes. His gaze swept her face.

She felt a tugging on her skirt but didn't want to look away just then.

"Adam would like to know if he can stable your new horse," Gawyn said.

Justina blinked. She saw his lips move, but it was a moment longer before she heard his words. "Oh." She dropped her arms from Gawyn's shoulders and took a step back from him, suddenly embarrassed. She tore her gaze from those hypnotic eyes to look down toward her skirt. Adam had been pulling on her dress to get her attention.

A boy with red hair and freckles raced up and took the reins, leading her mare away.

Justina watched the boy go. Her new horse! She felt as if a present was being taken away, but the thought was ridiculous.

"She'll be stabled. We'll get her when you leave."

Justina couldn't take her eyes from her brown and white horse, worried for the mare's welfare.

Adam stomped his foot slightly but whirled toward the castle in excitement. He couldn't remain angry for long. There was too much to see.

Gawyn chuckled, drawing her attention. "I remember coming to Acquitaine for the first time." He looked around the castle. "It can be overwhelming." He swiveled his head to her with his bright brown eyes twinkling. "It's always crowded and wherever you look, there is always movement. It's hard to find space to collect your thoughts."

Justina nodded in agreement. She felt breathless and wasn't certain if the reason was the castle or the man standing before her.

A child raced by after a goose, rustling Justina's skirt.

Gawyn eased her aside, out of the boy's way. "Come. I'll show you the spot I go when I need to get away from the crowds."

Justina glanced at Adam to make sure he was following them.

Her brother skipped happily after them. Justina hurried to Gawyn's side. "Where is it?"

"It's much quieter than the inner ward, I can tell you that. It reminds me of where I grew up. A little." He led them through the inner ward to the far wall, the wall all the way at the back of the castle. It was quieter, but not silent. In the corner, loud barking erupted from numerous dogs as they approached.

Justina looked at Gawyn. "This is it?"

Gawyn grinned at her; that sideways smile made her

heart skip a beat. "Adam," he called. The boy rushed to his side. "See that man there?" Gawyn pointed to a stocky, dark haired man with brown breeches, torn at the knee, and a brown tunic. "Go and ask him about the puppies."

"Puppies?" Adam wondered, his eyes grew large in excitement.

"One of our hunting dogs recently had puppies. I'm sure he'll show you."

Adam raced over to the man and spoke to him. The man lifted his gaze to Gawyn and waved slightly.

Gawyn nodded to him.

The man led Adam into the kennels.

"This way," Gawyn said.

Justina hesitated. "What about Adam?"

"We'll get him on the way back."

"The way back?" Justina echoed in confusion. She didn't like leaving Adam, but her curiosity got the better of her and she followed Gawyn into a large tower on the corner. She was sure it was the guard tower. "Are we allowed in here?"

Gawyn smiled at her. "I am the captain of the guard. I can go anywhere I want."

His grin was contagious, like a little boy in a room filled with sweets. They moved up one flight of stone stairs and then turned a corner and continued up more stairs. Three times they did this until Gawyn stopped before a door. His brown eyes twinkled in merriment as he gazed at her. He slowly opened the door.

A walkway stretched out before her. It lined the wall all the way across to the other guard tower. Justina stepped out onto the wooden planks. She looked down. Far below them, she saw the kennels, but she couldn't hear the barking.

The wind blew gently, rustling her hair. She pushed a strand away from her face, marveling at how quiet it was here. There were no sounds of the crowds, no merchants hollering, no animals barking or neighing.

"Better?" Gawyn asked.

"Too bad the view isn't better," she joked. "But yes, this is wonderful."

Gawyn took her hand and pulled her to one of the merlons. "This is Acquitaine." He put his hands on her shoulders and turned her so she was looking between the crenels, away from the castle. "We try to please."

Justina gasped at the sight. Mountains rose in the distance; the river rushed by before them reflecting their snow-capped peaks in its glistening water. The sun was setting, bathing the lands in a soft red glow. It was magnificent. So beautiful. So...

"Better?"

Justina couldn't answer. It was the most beautiful landscape she had ever seen. She glanced back at Gawyn. And he was the most handsome man she had ever seen. For a moment, she couldn't tear her gaze from his. Words escaped her. Her gaze swept his face. Strong square clean-shaven jaw, generous mouth, a straight proud nose, and his eyes. Oh, those eyes made her knees weak. She could see intelligence in them and a bit of humor. It wasn't what she could see in them, but how intense his gaze was when he looked at her. As if she were the center of the world, more beautiful than the view. "It's magnificent," she whispered.

He took her hand again and she was suddenly aware of the way it engulfed hers, warm and strong. He jumped up on the edge of the crenel, all the while holding her hand.

Her heart flinched. "No," she said, panicked. "Get

down from there."

He gently tugged her. "I'll help you."

"As I'm falling?" she asked and pulled her arm free. She shook her head. "I like the view from right here." Of course, looking up, she did have a grand view…of his rounded bottom.

He shrugged and leaned back against the merlon, his arms crossed. He looked out toward the mountains and for a long moment said nothing.

Justina followed his stare. The wind worked its way through the strands of her hair. She pushed them back from her eyes, not wanting to miss one second of the marvelous sight.

Gawyn inhaled. "I come up here to get away. When it all seems too much."

She looked at him positioned precariously on the edge of the crenel. He seemed so strong, so confident. "It's hard to believe there is anything you can't handle."

He glanced down at her, his hair falling forward. "Says a girl who took me down to the ground the first time we met."

"I…" she stuttered for a moment before clamping her lips closed. Her father had taught her the move. It was for defense. She shrugged. "I didn't know you. You could have been a robber."

He jumped down to her side. "How did you do it?"

Justina rolled her eyes. "I put my leg behind yours and pushed. It really wasn't that hard."

"How did you learn to do that?"

She couldn't look him in the eye. She shouldn't have been able to push over the captain of the guard. "I was the daughter of a rather overprotective father who worried about me wandering around the countryside. He wanted me to be able to take care of myself."

Gawyn leaned back against the wall of the castle. "What else did he teach you?"

Justina inhaled, thinking about all her father had taught her. "How to survive in the forest by eating what nature offered. How to hide in the forest. How to cover my tracks." She shrugged.

Gawyn laughed aloud. "That's not typical training for a young farm woman."

"I suppose not."

"Have you ever had to use any of your training?"

Justina cocked an eyebrow at him. "You mean beside you?"

Gawyn smiled full out.

Justina's heart did a small leap. He was gorgeous. She loved the sound of his laughter; she loved the way the sun shone onto his brown hair creating gold highlights. "I suppose not." She lifted her chin. "But I'm glad I had the training."

Gawyn's eyes narrowed slightly. "I'd like to see what you know. Perhaps I can add to your training."

"Why?"

"I'd like to know that you are protected, that you can defend yourself. I know what's out there. I know that not all of it is good."

Her smile slowly faded. Like an assassin. She realized he was not speaking about the monster living in the castle, but about barbarians bordering Acquitaine. "Like the Hungars." Justina considered his offer. She could learn more defensive moves, maybe even teach them to Adam. But strangely, it wasn't learning that was so appealing to her, it was the chance to be alone with Gawyn. She found it strangely thrilling. She agreed with a nod.

Gawyn's gaze swept her face slowly like a gentle caress.

Justina felt a strange heat blossoming over her cheeks and she looked away at the view again.

"We've missed the evening meal, but I'm certain we can find food in the kitchens, not that Joy will be happy to see us, but she will make sure you have something to fill your stomach."

Justina turned to him, opening her mouth to object, but he continued.

"I'd like to escort you around the castle, if you'd like. Unless you are too exhausted from the ride."

Justina grinned. "I'm not sure Adam will sleep the entire time he is here."

Gawyn nodded in understanding and led her back the way they had come. "I will introduce you to Lord Damien and Lady Aurora on the morrow."

CHAPTER 5

They took their time to eat a trencher bowl of bread filled with pork and apples, which of course, was delicious. Gawyn had never encountered a cook like Joy. No matter how much she protested the late comers, she lived for the praise, which Gawyn was only too happy to heap on her. After a quick wave of dismissal from Joy, Gawyn led Justina and Adam into the corridor.

Torches flickered on the walls, casting light over the entire corridor.

"That was amazing!" Adam exclaimed, rubbing his stomach. "What were those crunchy things?"

"Apples," Gawyn said with a grin. He remembered well his first taste of fruit. It was here at Acquitaine. "If you are tired, I can show you to your rooms." He knew full well that Adam was not close to being tired.

Adam looked askance at Justina.

"We'd hate to burden to you," Justina said.

"You are never a burden," Gawyn admitted. He couldn't look away from her large brown eyes. He liked the way the blush crept over the gentle curve of her cheeks.

"Can we see the pups again?" Adam asked.

"He's always wanted one," Justina said.

Gawyn nodded. "Of course." He led the way down the corridor and out the iron bound wooden doors into the night. The darkness was overwhelming now, the slitted moon the only light.

Justina tripped over a rise in the road and Gawyn caught her arm to steady her.

Adam raced ahead of them.

"Are you alright?" Gawyn asked softly.

"I'm sorry. I didn't see –"

"It's very dark back here." He kept his hand beneath her arm for support. She didn't object. Gawyn felt a strange flutter in his chest. He mentally shook his head. Yes, he enjoyed her company, but he had to keep in mind why she was here. "You live with your Uncle. Where is your father?"

"He died."

"I'm sorry."

She shook her head. "I was fifteen. It was long ago."

"How did he die?"

She turned to look at him with a questioning and suspicious slant to her eyes. "Why are you so interested in my father?"

Gawyn shrugged. "I want to get to know you. Adam is important to you, so I wanted to learn more about your family."

This seemed to pacify her. She looked after Adam who had run ahead. "Adam is important. He and Uncle Bruce are the only family I have left. If something happened to them…" She looked down.

Gawyn felt a deep urge to comfort her. Not for information, not for selfish reasons, but to ease her fear. He took her hand and squeezed it. "Adam is safe in Acquitaine."

She looked at their mingled hands, but made no move to pull away. Her brow furrowed and she looked toward Adam again. "I will keep him safe."

"As will I," Gawyn vowed. And he meant it.

She looked up at him. The sliver of moon reflected in her dark eyes. Gratitude glimmered in her orbs. Suddenly, she lifted up on the tips of her toes to press a kiss to Gawyn's cheek.

The world stopped for just that moment when her soft lips touched his grizzled cheek. His heart skipped a beat, his breath hitched. She pulled back and lifted her hand to his cheek. "Thank you."

Every instinct he had wanted to pull her against him and kiss her lips. Every instinct wanted to feel her body along the length of his. Instead, he nodded like a dim-witted young page.

She turned away and the moment was lost. He shook his head and ran his hand through his hair, wondering how brainless he would have been if she had kissed him on the lips.

It was very late when Gawyn led them up a spiral set of stone stairs. The castle was quiet, they only saw one servant moving through the corridors.

Justina glanced at Adam. He stifled a yawn. It had been a long day for him, but he would never admit he was tired. Not here.

"Where are we going?" Adam asked.

"To your chambers," Gawyn said. "They are on the

second floor."

Justina almost missed a step. "Here?" she asked. "In the castle?"

Gawyn glanced over his shoulder. "Where else would guests stay?"

Justina thought they would stay in an inn or perhaps with the servants, but never in the castle. "We shouldn't be sleeping in the castle. That is for noblemen."

Gawyn stopped and turned to her.

Justina almost collided into him.

"You are guests of Lord Damien and Lady Aurora. They would have my head if I didn't see to your accommodations." He continued up the stone stairs.

Justina scowled and followed. She was uneasy being such an esteemed guest. She was only a farmer, certainly not worthy of staying in the castle. And why was she here? To thank Lady Aurora for the horse and the protection. Her scowl deepened. Because Gawyn had told Lady Aurora of their plight. Because he had followed her and Adam from Acquitaine. Because the monster had told him to. Yes. This all came about because of the man who had killed her father. She couldn't forget that.

Even when Gawyn led them down a corridor and stopped before a door, she told herself that she must remember. But it was difficult because her mind continued to return to the way his skin felt beneath her kiss. Gawyn had been so kind to them and Adam adored him.

"You are guests here," he said softly, his hand on the iron handle of the door.

And then Gawyn swung the door open. Justina's mouth dropped open in surprise. The room was as big as two of their entire crucks. Against the far wall, two windows were curtained with rich red draperies, between them an elaborate tapestry hung depicting a hunting scene. A small fire burned in a hearth near a massive bed. Surely, five people could sleep in it comfortably! Perhaps she would have to share the room and the bed with others. Across from the hearth, to her right, an ornate wooden garderobe stood. The ceiling stretched high over their head.

Adam rushed past her into the room. "Gah!" He looked up at the ceiling, spinning.

"I will have Linda come up and bring a bath if you would like to use it. She will see to any of your needs," Gawyn said.

Adam stopped spinning. "Who's Linda?"

Gawyn grinned. "One of the servants here at Acquitaine."

"No. We don't need servants," Justina explained quickly.

"It's difficult to carry up the pails of water to heat your bath by yourself," Gawyn said.

"Bath?" Adam gawked. "I don't want a bath."

"All guests in the castle bathe. You have to look your best when I present you to the Lord and Lady of Acquitaine."

"Maybe you just stink," Justina said and laughed.

Adam lifted his arm and inhaled deeply.

Gawyn's look softened as he turned to Justina. "Will this room do for the two of you?"

Justina could only stare. It was more than enough for the two of them! She nodded because she could do nothing else.

"Very well. I will find Linda." He turned to depart the room.

"You're leaving?" Justina asked and was surprised at

the disappointment in her voice.

"I will return in the morning to present you to Aurora and Damien."

Adam thumped her shoulder. "He is the Captain of the Guard. He has to train the men and make sure that the castle is protected."

Gawyn smiled at him.

Justina's heart melted. She knew this, but she had never been able to sleep in a strange place the first night. And this luxury was the strangest of all.

Gawyn looked at her with a sincere gaze. "I am glad you came."

Warmth blossomed inside of Justina. She grinned back at him. She was glad she came, too.

Early the next morning, Gawyn approached Justina's room. He was surprised at how excited he was to see her. It was strange. He never felt this way about anyone. And a farm girl? But he knew there was more to her. Besides the way she watched over her brother, she was hiding a secret. Damien had told him she had said 'I know you'. It didn't matter. Damien had asked him to find out how she knew him. His brother had not said he couldn't enjoy his time with her.

As he approached the room, he heard loud shouts and quickened his step to the door. He paused, listening. It didn't sound like they were shouts for help. No. Giggles were laced between the shouts.

Gawyn knocked on the door.

Silence.

That made him uneasy. Where they in trouble?

"Justina? I'm coming in."

Scurrying sounded from the other side of the door.

Apprehensive, Gawyn eased the door open. Justina sat in a chair with her back to him near the hearth. Adam was at her side, holding a tray of grapes. His eyes were wide and his lips pressed tightly together. Linda, the dark-haired servant, was on her hands and knees beside Justina, frozen. Gawyn's gaze swept the room quickly for other threats, but there were none. He scowled as he stepped in, closing the door slowly behind him.

Adam giggled.

Linda reached for something on the floor and captured it in her hand.

Gawyn scanned the ground. Grapes spread across the floor around Justina's chair. "Good morn," Gawyn greeted. He was certain there was no threat, but he was very curious as to what they were doing.

Linda sat up, her brown skirt cupped with a heaping number of grapes in it. "Good morn, Captain."

"Good morn," Adam chorused in.

Justina mumbled something.

Gawyn took a step toward them. "Is the food to your liking?"

Adam fought a grin. "Very much."

Justina nodded, but still would not turn to him.

Linda picked up another grape and deposited it in her skirt.

"Was there an accident?"

Adam laughed, but cut his guffaw short as Justina looked at him.

"No, sir," Linda said. "Just some…spilled grapes."

Gawyn looked from Linda on her knees picking up

grapes, to Adam holding the tray, to the back of Justina's head. He crossed the room and bent to help Linda pick up the grapes.

"That's not necessary, sir," Linda said softly.

Gawyn smiled at her. He looked up at Justina who had turned away from him to Adam and was gesturing subtly. Gawyn placed the last grape into Linda's cupped skirt and rose, his curious gaze on Justina. He could only see the side of her face, but her cheek looked swollen and distended. "Justina…?"

She turned toward him, keeping her chin lowered so her dark hair fell forward to hide her face.

Gawyn stepped before her. He cupped her chin with his finger and lifted it.

Justina's entire mouth and cheeks were engorged like a squirrel preparing for hibernation. Her eyes met his and her cheeks flamed red.

"How many?" Gawyn asked.

Justina cocked her head to the side in confusion.

"How many grapes?"

Justina groaned, and her shoulder slouched.

"We were going for ten!" Adam exclaimed. "She almost did it!"

Gawyn glanced at Linda to find her head bowed, but a grin on her lips.

Gawyn cupped his hand near Justina's chin. "So, you must have been able to hold nine," he said to Adam.

Adam nodded, beaming with pride.

One grape slid from Justina's mouth, then another and another, until they were in a wet pile in Gawyn's hand. Gawyn deposited them in Linda's skirt.

"Nine was the most I've ever done!" Adam said,

handing the tray to Linda.

Gawyn wiped his hand on his sleeve. He patted Adam on the head. "Well done."

Justina stood. "I'm so sorry."

"There's no need to apologize," Gawyn admitted. "But I have to admit, when I entered the room, this was one of the last things I expected to find."

Justina nodded guiltily.

"He dared you, didn't he?" Gawyn wondered.

Justina grinned. "I just couldn't let him get away with being the reigning grape champion."

"Plus, I dared her." Adam smiled.

Gawyn nodded in understanding. He and Damien had played few games when they were young, but they were close. As close as Adam and Justina. "We shouldn't keep the Lord and Lady waiting."

Gawyn led them through the hallways toward the Great Hall. Adam regaled him of everything that happened the night before. Justina was silent, letting her brother talk. But she watched. The hallway, the people they passed.

They entered the back of the room quietly. They were late and had to stand at the back of the line, which was near the large double doors. It looked like Aurora had made progress in hearing the petitions and arguments, but Gawyn wasn't sure if they would make it to the front of the line before the day's hours were up. That was one thing Damien had insisted on. That Aurora keep hours for hearing her people's troubles. It took a lot out of her and he didn't like to see her so tired.

Villagers, freemen, and merchants packed the room, standing in small clusters near the tall stone walls.

Gawyn liked to sit in during the judgements and

listen. He got to hear a lot of what was going on in the city. Many times, the troubles stemmed from arguments between neighbors. But there were other times when there were security issues that directly involved him. He stood in the line, his hand resting over the pommel of his sword.

Aurora sat in a chair at the front of the hall, on a small platform three stairs above the main floor. Damien stood beside her. It wasn't long before Damien locked gazes with Gawyn. Gawyn nodded slightly to him, almost imperceptibly. Damien's gaze moved away, sweeping the crowd. Always searching the crowd, watching, to protect his lady.

They moved forward. Gawyn glanced at Justina. He still wondered how she knew Damien. He hoped for her sake that it wasn't his past. That she hadn't seen something she shouldn't have. She was straining to see the front of the room where Damien and Aurora were. Her eyes narrowed slightly. "Is this what you expected?" Gawyn asked softly.

Justina glanced at him. "Nothing is what I expected."

"Acquitaine can be overwhelming. But I am here to help you." Gawyn smiled in reassurance.

Her return smile lit her face, making her eyes shine with an inner light, making her entire face beam like some sort of beacon.

Beautiful. Simply beautiful. He had never met a woman like her, a woman that could sneak up on him, a woman that could pin him to the ground. A woman so full of life and conviction and surprises.

She turned back to the front of the room.

Gawyn followed her gaze. Near the platform where Aurora sat, Gawyn spotted a colorful garment. He stepped away from Justina to get a better view.

A man with a thick mustache was speaking earnestly. A slender woman with bare feet stood beside him. Gypsies. There had been reports of the gypsies seducing village men and dancing for coin. The villagers did not like the foreign gypsies. They were viewed as outsiders and, therefore, untrustworthy.

Gawyn shifted to hear Aurora's proclamation, although he had not heard the complaint from the gypsies.

"You may conduct your activities at market. You are welcomed inside the city walls to purchase necessary items," Aurora stated.

A murmuring trickled through the gathered crowd in the Great Hall.

The gypsy man bowed. "Thank you, Lady Aurora."

The gypsies were happy with this. The crowds in the city would not be. This was not the end of it. Even though it was a fair ruling, the villagers saw Acquitaine as their home and didn't want the foreigners in it. Still, the gypsies had to make a living. It would be an unpopular decision.

Gawyn watched the man and woman walk passed them toward the rear doors. Even the way they moved was foreign, languid, and sexy.

They moved up the center aisle as the next person presented their troubles to Aurora.

Suddenly, a commotion behind them caused Gawyn to whirl. Five men dressed in animal furs were pushing their way to the front of the room, shoving peasant and noble aside.

Gawyn recognized the Hungars immediately. He gently guided Justina and Adam to the side of the room without taking his eyes from the men. "Leave the room. Go out into the hall and wait for me there."

Justina didn't argue. She grabbed Adam's arm and exited through the great double doors they had entered through.

Gawyn skirted the wall and moved toward the raised dais where Aurora sat. Damien had already stepped down a stair, and stood before her protectively. The guards moved immediately to defensive stances. No one had drawn weapons, yet.

The Hungars stopped just before the stairs. They were all tall, and beefy, wearing animal pelts for clothing. Swords and axes hung from their belts.

"There is a protocol here," Aurora told them. "You must wait for your turn."

"We don't wait," one of the men responded in a gruff tone. The pelt of a bear draped over his shoulders; a necklace of fangs hung about his neck. His brown hair was stringy and greasy and hung past his shoulders. A scar ran from just below his left eye down to his chin. "For anyone."

"What do you want, Hogar?" Damien demanded.

"You put puny men on our lands."

Damien cast a quick glance at Gawyn for acknowledgement.

Gawyn shook his head. The soldiers were not on Hungar lands.

Damien looked back at Hogar. "They are on Acquitaine lands. Maybe you've forgotten where your borders are."

"We forget nothing. Least of all how weak you are."

Aurora stood and walked up to Damien's side. "We don't want war, Hogar. But my people will be protected."

"You're a pretty girl," Hogar grunted as the men around him laughed lustily. "We follow no woman's orders.

No matter how her tits jiggle."

Damien jerked forward, but Aurora caught his arm to restrain him.

Hogar chuckled. "You should visit Hungars to see what real men do for their women."

Damien's jaw clenched, but other than that, he appeared relaxed.

Gawyn knew that was when Damien was most dangerous. Every muscle in his body tensed, ready.

The soldiers and guards around him all had their hands on the pommels of their swords, ready for battle.

Hogar's gaze quickly moved over the armed soldiers which outnumbered his men three to one. His grin slipped. "I come to tell you to remove your men from our lands."

"And I tell you that my men are not on your lands." Damien snarled.

Gawyn saw the signal a second before Damien moved. Damien's left hand fisted. It was a sign that all the soldiers knew. Close in.

Suddenly, there was a flurry of movement. Gawyn drew his weapon and the all of the Acquitaine soldiers rushed forward. Gawyn placed the tip of his weapon to the throat of the Hungar standing beside Hogar before he could even pull his axe free of his belt.

Damien had Hogar pinned to the ground, an arm around his neck, his face smashed into the stone floor. He leaned toward him, whispering in his ear. Only Hogar heard what he said.

Hogar struggled for a long moment but could not escape Damien's hold.

Gawyn's gaze slid over the rest of the Hungar's. All had numerous weapons pointed at them. None were moving.

"Get off me," Hogar commanded.

Damien didn't move. He looked up at one of the men. "Rupert."

The soldier nodded

"See to it that Hogar and all of his men are escorted from Acquitaine lands."

"Aye, m'lord," Rupert answered.

Lithe and dangerous, Damien stood from Hogar, moving quickly out of his reach.

Hogar climbed to his feet. His upper lip trembled with rage. "We go where we want. When we want."

"You are *going* to leave Acquitaine," Damien said. "And you are not *going* to return."

Hogar's eyes widened in outrage. His lips curled with hatred, his teeth ground. Around him and his men, soldiers from Acquitaine moved forward, blocking all ways out except the large double doors at the back of the room. Hogar stood still for a tense moment. His gaze burned into Damien with a molten hatred. Finally, he whirled and led his men from the room. At least twenty Acquitaine soldiers followed them.

Aurora moved to Damien, she stroked his shoulder and he turned to her, capturing her hand in his. They locked gazes for a long moment. Aurora stroked his cheek and took a deep breath.

Gawyn moved to Damien's side. "If you feel like fighting, you should do it outside."

"How the devil did they get in here?" Damien demanded, ignoring his quip.

"I'll check on it," Gawyn replied, but he looked toward the door for Justina.

"Go with them, Gawyn. Take two squadrons of

soldiers and make sure they are off our lands. I'll have Sir Robert talk to the outer wall guards."

Gawyn turned to Damien. "I have Justina and her brother at the castle."

"Justina?" Damien repeated, in confusion.

"The girl who lives on the outer lands. In Auch. The one Aurora said to take men and protect. I think Hogar has mistaken those lands for his."

Damien cursed quietly. "Escort the Hungars. I'll have someone else entertain them until you return."

"Damien," Gawyn warned. He knew how distracted Damien was with the Hungars. He knew a girl was not his top priority. He would forget about her.

"I'll do it," Aurora said softly. "I'll find her, Gawyn. I'll make sure she is taken care of."

Gawyn smiled at her. He knew Aurora would take care of Justina. "Thank you. Tell her I'll see her when I come back." He jogged after the retreating soldiers.

Damien scowled slightly, unsure what to make of his brother's sudden interest in the simple girl. He glanced at Aurora.

"Are you alright?" she asked him, her fingers trailing lightly reassuringly over his arm.

Damien frowned fiercely and glanced at the double doors the Hungars had left through. "They will not insult you."

Aurora grinned. "I care not what they say. They words are empty."

Damien fumed silently. "I don't like them looking

you."

She tilted her head to the side. "You don't like anyone looking at me."

It was true. But he especially didn't like those barbarians looking at her.

"You frightened me," she admitted quietly.

For that he was sorry. He brought her hand to his lips and pressed a kiss to her knuckles. "I'll try not to do that again."

"Thank you."

"As long as Hogar never enters Castle Acquitaine again."

"Then we must make sure he doesn't," she agreed.

"Gawyn will see him out of Acquitaine and back to his lands. But that won't stop them." He looked down at her beautiful full lips. "I want you to stay inside the castle for the rest of the day."

Aurora lifted her gaze to him, casting those magnificent blue eyes on him. "You think I'm in danger?"

"I'd feel better knowing you were safe in the castle until the Hungars are out of Acquitaine."

She leaned forward and pressed a kiss to his cheek. "Then for today, I will stay in the castle."

Justina stood in the hallway, watching as people passed obscuring her view of the double doors to the Great Hall. Adam stood beside her, leaning back against the wall.

She had seen the Hungars emerge and a large group of soldiers follow them out the door. She had not seen Gawyn. Two noble women exited the room, speaking amongst themselves.

"Those Hungars are barbarians," the one with the green dress said.

"And dirty. They are disgusting," the other said. "Imagine them speaking to Lady Aurora like that."

They strolled passed Justina.

Adam sighed at her side. "I wish I could have stayed."

Justina stared at the door. "The captain wanted us safe. I'm sure he'll be out any moment." But she was beginning to think he had forgotten about them. It had been a long while since they had left the room, or what seemed like a long while. She found herself twisting her hands, worried for Gawyn's safety.

"I wasn't afraid," Adam said bravely.

Justina swung her gaze to him in disbelief. "You weren't? Those Hungars are fierce and bloodthirsty. Did you see the axe the one had? It was the size of your entire body! Be thankful that Gawyn told us to wait for him in the hall. We don't want to be anywhere near them."

Adam shucked an imaginary rock. "I'm not afraid," he repeated, but his voice lacked conviction.

Justina took a deep breath. She looked down the hall. She wasn't sure how to get back to the inner ward, let alone her horse. What if Gawyn didn't come back? What if he forgot about them? Would they be stuck wandering the halls of this massive castle forever? Justina looked at the door again. He was taking a long time. Maybe she should peek inside the Great Hall and see if Gawyn was still there. So many people had come out of the room.

Suddenly, Lady Aurora exited the room, followed by four soldiers. Justina couldn't help but inhaling at her beauty and grace. Her dress was a beautiful white with golden embroidery. Her golden hair fell in waves around her shoulders covered by a thin veil. She paused in the doorway and looked first left then right until her gaze settled on them. A slow, warm grin spread over her lips.

Adam gasped as she approached, pushing himself from the wall.

"Are you Justina?" Lady Aurora asked.

Justina opened her mouth. It wasn't that Lady Aurora was scary or unapproachable. It was that she was so beautiful. Her blond hair reflected golden light. It hung over her shoulders in perfect waves, covered by a shimmering veil. Her eyes were large and blue, like the color of a rare sapphire. Justina couldn't recall a woman who was more stunning. She closed her mouth and nodded.

Aurora smiled. "I remember you from the village. I'm sorry that Damien frightened you."

Damien? Justina's mind echoed. But she pushed the thought away and suddenly remembered her manners. She fell into a deep curtsey before her. She was honored that Lady Aurora remembered her from the village square!

"Gawyn was taken away on business. He requested you wait for him."

"Wait for him?" Justina echoed, rising from her curtsey.

"Yes. You will wait, won't you?"

"Of course!" Adam called.

"How long will he be?"

Aurora looked at her with sympathy. "I'm afraid most of the day. I'm certain we can find entertainment for you."

Justina scowled. She would love to wait for Gawyn,

but she couldn't be away from Uncle Bruce and the farm for long. And then, she remembered the reason she came. "Lady Aurora, I wanted to thank you for the horse. It was generous of you."

"I was disturbed at the raids happening so close to you. I don't want you to be in danger."

"The captain brought a lot of guards to protect us!" Adam exclaimed excitedly.

Justina blinked. Her brother! "My lady," she said quietly, "this is my brother, Adam."

Aurora turned to Adam. She folded her hands before her and regarded him with an appreciative grin. "What a marvelous little man. You shall grow into a great knight, I am sure."

Adam beamed and puffed out his chest.

Justina had never seen him so quiet. Lady Aurora certainly cast a spell over all of them.

"Will you stay?" Aurora asked Justina. "Gawyn would be so upset if you left."

Justina felt so uncomfortable, so torn. She knew that they should return to Auch and Uncle Bruce, and yet, she didn't want to disappoint Gawyn, not after everything he had done for them. She glanced at Adam.

He put his hands together as if praying.

With a small sigh, she nodded. "I suppose one more day would be acceptable."

Adam whooped.

Aurora smiled. "I'm very glad you've chosen to spend one more day with us. I'm sure Gawyn will be happy, also."

"I'm happy!" Adam exclaimed.

"Have you eaten?" Aurora began walking down the

corridor.

Justina and Adam followed. Justina was afraid that if she didn't, she would be lost in the castle forever.

"Grapes," Adam said.

Justina grinned. She glanced back at the guards that followed.

"I trust your accommodations are satisfactory?" Aurora said.

"They're so big!" Adam stated in awe.

"Yes," Justina said. "They are more than satisfactory. It's all so generous of you to welcome us like this."

"You are guests here," Aurora said kindly. "I hope that you will return often and report upon the conditions of the borders. You will be our border ambassadors."

Border Ambassadors. Justina liked that. It was an important title.

"Border Ambassadors," Adam repeated with an impressed tone.

"I will," Justina promised. "*We* will. We would be honored. You've done so much for us already. We'll make regular trips now that we have a horse."

"Thank you for the horse!" Adam piped in.

"You're welcome, Adam," Aurora said.

"I can't thank you enough for sending soldiers to guard us in Auch."

"I wish you had told me earlier. I do not want any of my people living in fear. I had no idea the Hungars were raiding our land."

Lady Aurora nodded at a nobleman with pointy-toed shoes who passed them as she walked down the hallway. "You live with your uncle?"

"Uncle Bruce!" Adam chimed.

"Uncle Bruce takes care of you?"

"Yes," Justina admitted.

"Where are your parents?"

"Mother died in childbirth a long time ago," Justina said. She didn't want to talk about her father, but she felt obliged. "And father is dead, also."

"He died when I was little," Adam added.

Aurora stopped and turned to them. "I am sorry. I know how hard it is to lose a parent."

Justina remembered hearing about the death of Aurora's father, Lord Gabriel. "I'm sorry about your father."

Aurora nodded. "Thank you."

Justina heard the pain in her voice and knew her agony was still fresh. She knew that pain and felt an instant kinship with her.

Aurora started down the corridor again. "How did your father die?"

Justina almost tripped. The question shouldn't have caught her off guard, but somehow it did. "An accident."

"Someone killed him," Adam added.

Justina threw him a stern look. She couldn't blame him, it wasn't a secret. He didn't know that their father's killer was somewhere in the castle. And for a moment, Justina had almost forgotten. She had basked in the honor and prestige of following the lady of the castle and forgotten what darkness lurked around one of these corners. They should not stay. And yet, she wanted to see Gawyn again.

"How horrible!" Aurora exclaimed. "Why would someone do that?"

Adam shrugged, turning to watch a knight in chain mail walk by.

Aurora glanced at Justina, meeting her gaze. "Was

the killer ever found?"

"No," Adam said softly.

Justina looked down at the stone floor, remembering. "He disappeared as quickly as he came."

"You saw it," Aurora whispered. She placed a comforting hand on Justina's arm. "How old were you?"

Justina shook her head. "It doesn't matter."

"If I ever see the murderer, I will run my dagger through his heart!" Adam proclaimed.

"You weren't there," Justina said softly. "You didn't see him."

"I know. But if I did..."

Justina lifted her gaze to see concern wrinkling Aurora's smooth brow.

"The world can be a dangerous place," Aurora said. "I'm glad you weren't hurt."

Justina could only nod. With the haunting image of the dark eyes of the murderer and her father's blood on her hands, a tremor coursed through her. The monster was here in Acquitaine, of that, she was certain.

CHAPTER 6

Aurora spent some time with Adam and Justina before she was called away. She left them with Linda to see to their needs. After speaking to the head cook about the evening meal, she hurried to find Damien. She had a horrible, sinking feeling. Her father had been murdered. And Gawyn had somehow known she needed a horse and men to guard the borders. Well, the borders was his job, but was it coincidence that she had seen Justina in the village square and Gawyn had taken a sudden interest in her? Or was it more likely that it all had something to do with Damien?

She knew Damien would be at the barracks, supervising the training of the men. She sent a messenger to find him and bring him back to her. She waited for him in her chambers. She sat in a chair, facing the hearth. The fire reminded her of so many things, dark things. Roke's castle in flames. Her father's death. She had endured much to be with Damien. And she loved him so. It frightened her every day that his past might come back to haunt them. The darkness of what he had been might return to break them apart.

She knew for certain an assassin had killed Justina's

father. The way the girl described him. 'He disappeared as quickly as he had come.' There was only one assassin that Aurora knew of. It couldn't be coincidence. Damien had to know.

She stood and began to pace before the hearth. She would protect Damien at all costs. The thought that someone might know who he had been…

The door opened, and Aurora whirled to see Damien entering. His strong gait, his powerful presence, should have eased her doubts. But this was her one fear, that someone would recognize him from his past. She met him halfway across the room, stretching her hands out to him.

He clasped her hands, his brow wrinkled with concern. "What is it?"

"Justina's father was killed by an assassin."

Damien straightened just a bit, his lips pressed into an even slash. His dark eyes stared into hers.

"Do you think…? Could it have been…?"

"I asked Gawyn to find out. I haven't had a chance to speak with him." He looked down in thought. "But the way she looked at me in the square…"

"Fearful," Aurora added. "I remember."

"I think there's a good chance…"

Aurora stepped into his warmth, pressing herself into the crock of his arm. For a long moment, she didn't say anything. She wanted to protect him so badly. He was no longer that killer. He was honorable and strong. Saved. Loved.

"She's just one person," he whispered into her hair.

Aurora pulled back, startled. "She was hurt by your actions. She is still hurting."

Damien's grip on her arms tightened. He nodded

once. "I know." There was regret in his dark eyes.

She had never asked him if he was sorry for what he had done. "Would you take it all back, if you could?"

"No."

"No?" She pulled away from him, angry and hurt at his callous answer. "But all those people you killed, and the families you hurt."

He stood, stoically, taking her reprimand. "I would not take one back. Because they all led me here, to you."

Her heart melted. Tears welled in her eyes. How could she not see?

"You are my life. You are my redemption. I had to travel through that darkness to reach you."

She reached for him, pressing her head against his chest as tears fell from her eyes. "I'm sorry. I'm sorry I couldn't reach you sooner."

He hugged her tightly, pulling her against him, pressing kisses to her wet cheeks.

She would never understand that part of his life, and he rarely spoke of it. But it was part of who he was. He had survived it and it had made him the man she loved. She looked up at him. "I'll talk to her."

"It won't matter what you say," Damien warned. He tucked a lock of her hair behind her ear. "You know that."

She did. She had discovered that Damien had killed her mother and she had rejected him with as much repulsion as Justina was doing. Only when her father explained to her that he was following orders, did she allow forgiveness into her soul. And, of course, by then it was too late for her. She was already in love with him. She lifted up on her toes and pressed a kiss to his lips. "She's afraid. There's still hope that she will see you for who you are now."

Damien dipped his head, kissing the soft part at the base of her neck.

Aurora wrapped her arms around his neck. "And I think Gawyn could make her understand."

Linda had shown them around the castle. During it all, Justina found it difficult not to look for Gawyn. She expected him around every corner, in every room. Why wasn't he back? Where was he?

As the sun began its downward descent in the sky, Linda led them back to their chambers where she presented Justina with beautiful dresses and said she could wear them. Wear them? She was afraid to touch them! But she couldn't resist. She ran her hand along the soft fabric, softer than the cotton smocks she always wore; softer than any material she had ever touched. She yanked her hand back. She couldn't wear any of these dresses! It wasn't right. She was not a noble. And yet... it might be the only chance she ever got to wear clothing like this, to pretend she was something more than a farmer.

She cringed. She couldn't wear the elaborate, beautiful clothing Linda had laid out on the bed. She looked down at her stained brown cotton dress. Then, she sighed, and her shoulders slumped. Linda had told her she and Adam would be dining at the head table with Lady Aurora. She couldn't wear what she was wearing now. She looked at the dresses. A thrill rushed through her as she made the decision.

Linda picked out a green velvet dress with beautiful red embroidery. It was much too fancy for her. But Justina had to admit she loved the dress. When Adam was being dressed behind a curtain, Justina spun around and looked at her reflection in a metal bowl. She didn't recognize the woman looking back. She looked like a princess. Her hair had been washed and combed out. It hung about her shoulders in dark waves. Her skirt whooshed around her legs when she walked. She had never, ever, been close to material like this, let alone got to wear it!

Adam emerged from the curtain with his head down. He pulled at the dark blue jupon. "I hate this," he grumbled.

Justina wanted to laugh at his awkwardness but choked it down. She knew exactly how he felt. "Just one night."

"What if I spill something on it?"

"Just be careful."

He scowled and tossed his head of dirty blonde hair to the side. He looked at her with a scowl etched into his brow, with wildness in his eyes. Like he was going to run. Like he wanted to run.

"Imagine what your princess will think of you!" Justina added quickly.

The wildness vanished from his eyes as they lit with hope. "Really? Do you really think she will like it?"

"Most certainly."

Adam didn't complain after that.

Linda led them to the Great Hall and Justina was grateful for that because she never would have found it without her guidance. The castle was, perhaps, as big as the entire village of Auch. Justina would have gotten lost after the first turn.

When they came to the Great Hall, Justina paused. Tables stretched before her on either side of the room and they were filled with men and women. Some wore commoners clothing, brown breeches and tunics. Beyond the commoners, the knights sat. They took up most of the tables. Before the head table were the nobles. Their glorious gowns and rich jupons proclaimed their heritage.

Linda moved up the middle aisle, Justina and Adam following. Nervously, their gazes shifted from side to side. The entire room echoed with raucous talking and laughter.

Linda guided them up to the head table, which was empty. She signaled they should take the two chairs near the center.

"Are we early?" Justina asked, feeling her stomach knot with discomfort.

"Lady Aurora and Lord Damien will be here shortly. You are not early."

Damien. Again, the name sent unease through her, but she couldn't explain why. Justina nodded, thanked Linda, and took one of the seats closest to the center chairs. Adam took the seat beside her.

Linda bowed and moved away.

Justina wished she wasn't the center of attention. She wished she wasn't at the front table. She didn't like the way the nobles were leaning in to talk to each other and casting glances her way. She looked at Adam. He was staring out over the crowd with wide eyed awe. He caught her staring and whispered, "This is grand!"

Justina smiled at her brother's enthusiasm. It was the only time she would ever be here, dining at the head table. She could do it for Adam. Still, she clenched her hands tightly in her lap. She gazed this way and that, her stare moving over the gathering, searching. Disappointment nestled in her chest. Gawyn was not here.

Suddenly, a murmur swept over the crowd and the conversation quieted. Lady Aurora walked up the center aisle, as royal and beautiful as an angel. Justina stared, as star struck as everyone else. The way Aurora moved, the stature of her body and the way she carried herself. She was stunning. And Justina wanted to be like her. She found herself sitting straighter in her chair, lifting her chin.

Aurora seemed oblivious to the way people looked at her. With adoration. With breathless fascination. She nodded greetings to some, smiled at others. She took her seat at Justina's side and for a moment, the silence lingered. Slowly, the people returned to their conversations. "I am sorry I am late."

Adam quickly moved to the seat next to Aurora.

Aurora smiled at him. "You look very handsome, Adam."

Justina knew Adam was infatuated. He had the attention of his princess, who told him he looked handsome. What more could his heart ask for? He opened his mouth, but nothing came out.

The servants emerged from the kitchens, carrying large silver trays with various meats and vegetables.

"Will Captain Gawyn be joining us tonight?" Justina wondered, perhaps a bit too excited.

Aurora stared at her for a long moment with bright blue eyes, as if seeing something in Justina she liked. "I do not think he will make it back in time. He had work to do."

Justina's face fell in discontentment. She hadn't realized how much she had looked forward to seeing him. "Oh."

"You will stay until he returns? I know he would be disappointed if you were not here."

"I..." Justina lowered her gaze to her lap where her hands were clenched nervously. She couldn't stay forever. Uncle Bruce needed their help on the farm. She and Adam should be returning to Auch, they had responsibilities. "I..."

Aurora reached out to put her hand over hers. "I know you have a lot to do in Auch."

Over Lady Aurora's shoulder, Justina locked eyes with Adam.

"You said we could stay one more day," Adam pleaded.

Justina sighed and nodded. "I did. Only one more day." She hoped Gawyn made it back, so she could... so she could what? He was Captain of the Guard. She was a farmer. She was being impractical thinking they could be anything.

Adam clenched his fist in a gesture of excitement. Aurora nodded in acceptance, but she had a pleased glint in her eyes that confused Justina.

Aurora suddenly turned, and Justina saw a dark-haired man at her side. She wasn't sure where he had come from; she hadn't seen him enter the room. Her throat clenched tight and she suddenly found it difficult to breathe. Tremors shot up her spine. Fear gripped her in a tight embrace.

It was the monster.

Justina froze as the monster bent to kiss Aurora's head. Her mind screamed in denial.

"Justina, this is my husband, Lord Damien," Aurora introduced.

He locked gazes with her.

Damien! her mind shouted. The monster. He was the one she had seen. Her mind instinctively turned back to that moment in time. She had accompanied her father to the market that day. He had said he had business to attend to. He always had business to attend to. It was the first day her father let Adam remain home alone.

Her father told her to run and get herself a tart. What a treat! A tart! He had given her coin, telling her he would meet her. He had to relieve himself. He kissed her forehead and she raced away as her father ducked behind a building. She returned, having eaten half the tart. She turned the corner...

Her father lay on his back in the dust of the street. A man dressed in black stood over him. He wiped a bloodied blade on the front of her father's tunic. When he stood, she saw him. She saw his face! And it was the same face she was staring at now.

It was a long moment before she realized he had spoken and the three of them were staring at her. Murderer! her mind screamed. But she knew she couldn't accuse him. He was a powerful lord and she a commoner. Tears filtered across her eyes. She felt helpless to move, to speak, to extract vengeance. He had killed her father. He had taken him from her.

"Are you alright?" Lady Aurora asked.

Justina tore her gaze from Lord Damien's dark one. "I'm sorry," she whispered. She couldn't stop the trembling in her voice. "I don't feel well." She couldn't stay here. Her hands were clenched into tight balls. She couldn't remain here for one more moment. She stood and whirled with such speed that she knocked her chair over. She didn't look back, but hurried from the head table, walking at a quick pace down the long aisle. The room wavered before her eyes; warmth descended over her like a blanket. She didn't see the knights stop to look at her. She didn't see the servant carrying the large tray that she almost ran into.

This was wrong. All of it was wrong. Lady Aurora didn't care about them, didn't care to protect them. She was plying them with sweets and pretty clothing and large rooms for her husband. She was trying to atone for what Lord Damien did by giving them a horse!

Her throat closed as she reached the door. Her stomach clenched tight and nausea rose in her mouth.

"Justina?"

She looked up to see Linda standing near her. Aurora had sent Linda, not to see to their needs, but to watch them. How gullible she had been! She had wanted to believe that her lord and lady wanted what was best for them. But why would they? They were nothing to them. Peasants. They had shown no interest before.

Linda lay a comforting hand on Justina's shoulder.

Justina yanked away from it. She didn't want to wear these tainted clothes. She trembled violently. "Show me back to my room." She just wanted to go home.

Justina paced the darkened room. The firelight from the hearth was the only light in the room. It washed over her as she stood staring at the snapping and hissing flames. Then, she whirled and stalked back into the darkness. She had quickly changed clothes back to her cotton dress and bodice. She hated the beautiful dress and the large room and even the sweets on the table. She hated Acquitaine. She hated Aurora for making her feel welcomed and safe. It had all been a ruse to protect her husband. And she had the coin to do it.

Justina turned and moved toward the light of the

hearth. She was only waiting for Adam. Once he came, they were leaving. Running. They would never, ever return here.

Where was Adam? What had they done to him? It had been at least an hour since she had left the Great Hall. She never should have left Adam with them. But she had been so sick at her discovery, that she just had to get away. She had left her brother. Her heart clenched, and she stormed to the door. If they hurt him, she would kill them. All of them!

She stopped. How was she going to do that? She had nothing. And they had everything. The Lord of Acquitaine had taken her father away from her. And now... Now, where was Adam?

She marched to the door. The door opened before her.

A shadow stood in the doorway, holding a limp Adam in his arms.

CHAPTER 7

Justina shrunk back, recognizing Lord Damien. Her heart lurched in terror as her eyes shifted to Adam and protectiveness washed over her. What had he done to Adam? She overcame her fear and reached out, ripping Adam from his arms.

"I was showing him around the castle," Damien explained, "and he fell asleep in the throne chair. He must have been more tired --"

"Stay away from him, you monster," Justina growled, wiping some of Adam's hair from his forehead and moving to the bed to lay him down.

Damien stood in the doorway for a long moment.

"I know who you are," Justina snapped, whirling on him. "I know what you did. You are a killer. A murderer."

Damien didn't move. He stood silently, a dark shadow lit by the dancing torchlight in the hallway behind him. "I didn't hurt him."

"Stay away from him!"

Another heartbeat passed before Damien nodded and left the room, softly closing the door.

Justina sat on the bed beside Adam. In the soft glow of the firelight, Adam's face looked pale. Her mind interposed the face of her dead father over Adam's. Her trembling hand had wiped her father's hair from his forehead, too. "Adam?" She didn't know what she would do if anything happened to her brother.

He moaned softly and opened his eyes sleepily. When he saw her, a grin spread over his lips. "You should have seen the barracks," he whispered.

Justina nodded as relief filled her. He was fine, just exhausted from so much excitement. "Shhh," she said softly. "Go to sleep."

"Can we stay another day?"

She wanted to leave as soon as possible, but how could she say no to her brother? He meant the world to her. "We'll talk about it tomorrow."

"I want to see the falcons..." His voice trailed off as he slipped into sleep.

Justina pulled one of the blankets over him. What was she going to do?

Monster. It was unnerving to hear the accusation here, in Acquitaine. Damien had come to believe he was more than that. He was loved by Aurora. That should be enough.

He entered the solar.

Aurora was bent over a table, studying a piece of parchment. She looked up as he entered, her face turning to joy. She slowly rose, and her happiness faded to concern. "What's wrong?"

"She knows." Damien looked away from her.

"Damien –" She reached out to touch him.

Damien pulled away, moving across the room to the hearth. He stared down into the dancing fire. "I knew this day would come."

"What day?"

"When my past would catch up with me. When someone would recognize me." He had been living on borrowed time, this life was too wonderful for him, almost a dream. He knew it couldn't last.

"She hasn't accused you of anything," Aurora reasoned. "Are you certain she knows it was you?"

Monster. "I'm certain."

"I shall speak to her. I am certain –"

"No." Damien didn't want Aurora to know any of the horrible murders he had committed in his other life. She already knew too much. "I will deal with it."

"Damien." She touched his shoulder, pulling him around to look at her. "You are my husband now. You are Lord of Acquitaine."

Damien scowled in confusion.

She touched his cheek with affection. "You are not the person you were. You will never be that person again. We will speak to her, together. Explain –"

"Explain what?"

Aurora's gaze swept his face.

"The only thing that matters to her is what I did. We could never explain. Not to her. And she will never understand."

Aurora brushed his cheek with her fingers. "We'll think of something."

Damien stared at her crystal blue eyes. She was a master of negotiation and compromise. A perfect diplomat.

What she didn't understand was that some people didn't want to compromise. He nodded. They would find a way. With Aurora, all things were possible. He knew that as a fact. Because she had changed him. She had made him into an honorable man. He grabbed her and pulled her into his embrace. "I love you." She was his life.

Gawyn had rode hard all night to be back at Acquitaine. He was tired, his steed was tired. They had accomplished the task of seeing the Hungars to the border. He had even waited until they disappeared in the darkness. Then, he had ridden with his men to Uncle Ben's farm to make sure he was unharmed. The men stayed there under Rupert's orders, but Gawyn wanted to be back at the castle.

Now, he thundered into Castle Acquitaine just after the sun rose. He didn't even wait for the stable boy to take the reins of his horse. He quickly dismounted, surprisingly anxious to see Justina. He just had this feeling that something was amiss. He walked into the keep. The entryway was overly crowded for that early in the morn. Someone must have just arrived at the castle or come back from a hunt. He scanned the crowd for Damien. His brother usually towered over the rest and was easy to spot, but there was no sign of him.

Gawyn spotted Aurora. Her face was bright with excitement. She was speaking to a noble girl, her hands clasping the girl's. He glanced toward the stairs where the chambers were.

"Gawyn!"

He turned toward Aurora's voice. For a brief

moment, he caught sadness in her eyes. Then, it was gone behind the familiar façade of strength and beauty. He moved over to her. "Gawyn, this is my cousin, Megan."

Gawyn was anxious to find Justina, but he bowed and greeted her cousin. He was amazed at how much she looked like Aurora. Their hair was the same golden waves. Their lips were similar, full, and luscious. It was their eyes that were different. Megan had brown eyes. And she was younger. Maybe three or four summers younger then Aurora. Inexperienced. "My pleasure, m'lady."

Megan smiled.

"This is our captain of the guard. Gawyn." Aurora linked her arm through Gawyn's. "He is Damien's brother." She looked at Gawyn and there was seriousness in her eyes. "Gawyn has just ridden from the borders of Acquitaine. Did all go well?"

"Yes, m'lady. Our guests were escorted without incident."

Aurora nodded. "Good. I hope you are not too tired this morn. I have further need of your services."

Gawyn glanced at Aurora. She was trying to hide something from her cousin.

"Adam would like to see the falcons before he leaves."

Tingles danced across the nape of Gawyn's neck. Justina was leaving? So soon? Something must have happened. He wanted to ask what had happened, but knew Aurora was hiding something from her guests. Gawyn turned to go.

"Gawyn," Aurora called.

Gawyn looked at her and there was anguish in her eyes.

"I'm sorry."

He was confused as to the reason, but her apology only added to his anxiety. What had happened? He nodded and hurried to the spiral stairway leading to the second floor, taking them two at a time. The closer he got, the more he wanted to see Justina. His heart pounded with worry. At least she was unharmed. But Aurora's apology concerned him. What had happened?

As he neared the door, he heard Adam's voice shouting, "I don't want to leave! You promised. One more day!"

He didn't hear Justina's response, it was too soft. They were leaving. Why? He had, Aurora and Damien had, done everything they could to make them feel comfortable and welcomed. He paused at the door, wondering if he should disturb them. He was afraid if he didn't knock, they would leave without saying goodbye. And he would never see her again. The thought was foolish. He knew where they lived. He could visit anytime. Still, the unease lingered. He lifted his hand to knock.

Justina opened the door. Her eyes widened at seeing him and then, her jaw clenched with anger.

Startled, Gawyn asked, "Is everything okay?"

She glanced back at Adam and then to him. "Fine. Why wouldn't it be?" she snapped.

Gawyn was stunned at the sharpness in her tone. "I've come to take Adam to see the falcons."

Justina straightened. "We're leaving."

Gawyn's eyebrows rose in surprise. "Without saying goodbye?"

Adam ducked beneath her arm. "She promised we could stay another day! And now, she lied to me."

Gawyn's gaze shifted to Justina. He didn't want to interfere in their family dispute, but he wanted her to stay. "I barely got to spend time with you."

"You did what you intended. You dropped us here and left."

Gawyn couldn't believe his ears. Was she angry that he had obligations? "Were you not taken care of?"

"I'm not a child who needs to be pampered."

"You're acting like one," Gawyn retorted.

Her mouth dropped at the insult.

Gawyn sighed. He ran a hand through his hair. He was tired. "I hurried back as fast as I could. I'm sorry I left you."

Justina nodded curtly, and her chin lifted. "You have no obligation to us. We're just commoners who live on the outskirts of your lands. That's all."

"They are not my lands," Gawyn corrected. Then, he shook his head. "Justina, I don't understand. What happened? Have I done something to upset you?"

"She got sick last night," Adam said. "It must have addled her brains."

"Adam!" Justina snapped.

"That is no way to speak to a lady," Gawyn reprimanded.

"She's not a lady," Adam whispered hotly and crossed his arms, disappearing into the room with a pout.

"If you'd like, I could escort your brother to see the falcons before you leave. That way, at least, he won't be angry with you."

Justina seemed to consider his idea. She lowered her gaze in thought.

Gawyn had no idea what had happened to make her

so angry. She didn't look sick. There were dark rings under her eyes. Maybe she didn't sleep well, but that was no reason to be so angry. No. Something had happened. He watched her for any clue.

She glanced back toward Adam and sighed. "I suppose that would be acceptable."

"Thank you, thank you, thank you!" Adam exclaimed, rushing forward, and throwing his arms around her waist.

Gawyn grinned at the boy, but he couldn't help but feel a swirling sadness inside of him. "I'd like for you to accompany us, but I will understand if you don't feel well and would rather stay in your room."

"It's not *my* room."

Again, Gawyn was taken aback at her tone. Her anger was incomprehensible. It seemed she was angry at everything except her brother. "My pardons. I meant in this room."

The furrow on her brow was testament to her unhappiness. She looked him over with a quick sweeping gaze. "When did you get back?"

Gawyn shook his head. "Just now. Literally. My horse is probably still in the ward."

"You haven't eaten yet?"

"It doesn't matter. This is more important."

He saw a softening in her lovely brown eyes and the furrowing in her brow smoothed. "We have sweets and fruit, if you'd like some."

Gawyn glanced over her shoulder and saw the table near the hearth was covered with bowls of fruit and trays of sweets. Then, he looked back at her. "Justina, I don't understand what I did to make you so angry. I'm sorry I had to leave. I really am. But the safety of Acquitaine is important to me. There are a lot of people who depend on me. And I won't let them down."

She looked away from him, but not before he noticed she was frowning again. Was that really what it was? That she felt he abandoned her?

"Will you come with us to see the falcons?" Gawyn asked.

She looked down for a long moment as if weighing her options. She glanced at Adam. "Yes. I will."

Satisfaction and joy bloomed in Gawyn's heart but beneath swirled despair.

Justina let Adam do all the talking. He had a hundred questions. She stayed behind them, trailing Gawyn and her brother. She was going to say no, that she didn't want to accompany them. But then she thought about Adam. She didn't want to leave him alone. Not after the terrible sight from last night. Seeing Adam's limp body in that monster's arms. It was horrifying. She wanted to know where Adam was every second of every day. That was the only reason she had accompanied them. It was dangerous, she knew. Because she couldn't allow herself to have feelings for Gawyn. He was loyal to the killer. She couldn't allow herself to get close to him.

Gawyn was exceptional with Adam. He easily answered all his questions, even the silly ones, without making Adam feel inadequate. Adam looked at him as if the moon rose and set with each word he said. It would be easy to open her heart to Gawyn. Adam had already done it. So, this was the last time she could come here with Adam. She couldn't let him get hurt. Not physically and not emotionally. He hadn't seen what she had seen. And he would certainly never understand the revenge she wanted desperately to extract.

Gawyn and Adam laughed together as one of the falcons swooped down low over their heads.

Justina gasped at the graceful way the bird flew, its wings barely batting, just gliding. Beautiful. The falcon swooped up and landed on a perch on the other side of the yard. In one of the open windows of the castle, she saw the monster watching them. Lord Damien leaned slightly over the window ledge, gazing downward. His black hair tossed over his shoulders in a gentle breeze. He looked menacing and dangerous. But suddenly behind him, the Lady Aurora appeared. She wrapped her arms around him and he hooked one of his arms around her waist to pull her close.

Justina cringed. How could she touch a killer? How could she love him? Didn't she know his hands had blood on them?

Aurora whispered something to the monster. He grinned and bowed his head. She lifted up and pressed her lips to his. The tenderness between them was touching.

"It's hard for Damien to be a lord. He wasn't raised as a noble." Gawyn had come up behind her.

"I know." Justina looked at Gawyn. "I mean, he doesn't look like a noble."

Gawyn narrowed his eyes slightly and Justina turned back to watch them.

"He loves her very much, doesn't he?" she asked.

Gawyn lifted his gaze to the window. "She is his world. She gave him a new life. I'm glad he found her."

Justina stared at them. He loved her as much as she

Laurel O'Donnell

loved her father. As much as she... She tore her gaze from them. He still had the one he loved. Her father was long gone. It wasn't fair.

She looked at Adam speaking to the falconer, an older man with a protruding stomach. She wet her lips and gritted her teeth, preparing herself. "You came to the farm that first night because Lord Damien sent you," she whispered so Adam didn't hear.

Gawyn nodded. "Yes. He asked me to ask you and Adam to dine at the castle."

Her suspicion rose, as did the agony. It had all been a ploy. "Was that the real reason he sent you?"

Gawyn turned to her. "Justina –"

"Why would he ask a couple of commoners to dine at the castle? Why us? No. He sent you to find out."

"To find out?" he repeated, confused.

She looked at him, desperately trying to keep her composure. She did so like him. "You work for Lord Damien."

"Yes."

She stared at his brown, trusting eyes. His strong chin. His furrowed brows. And her heart cracked. "Isn't it more likely that he sent you to see what I knew?"

"Knew about what?"

"Stop it," she commanded. "Don't treat me like that. I fell in the street and I recognized him. I said I knew him. Isn't it more likely that he sent you to see what I knew?"

CHAPTER 8

Gawyn stared at Justina. Her anguished eyes, her stubborn raised chin. His heart cried out. He didn't want to lie to her. "Yes," he sighed. "I never intended to hurt you. I just wanted to find out how you knew him. Those were my orders."

"Why didn't you tell me?"

Gawyn shook his head. "He is a good ruler. I wanted you to see him –"

Adam rushed up to them, interrupting. "Did you see how the falcon sat on my arm? Did you?"

Justina nodded.

Gawyn saw how her chin quivered. He wanted to explain to her, but she quickly turned her attention to her brother.

"We have to go now."

"I'll be fine," Aurora promised Damien as she sat in a chair in the solar. Her lady's maid, Anna, a dark haired young woman, combed Aurora's golden locks to shining perfection. "You know I would love to have you come, even though you don't like picnics. But I know you have to fortify the castle against the Hungars."

"Exactly why I don't want you leaving." He watched her with crossed arms as he leaned back against the wall. He didn't like the idea of a picnic. Not now. He shook his head, grimacing and came forward to sit in the chair beside her. "Nothing is more important than you." His sunshine. His light. He would be lost without her.

She turned to him with genuine respect and understanding. "Megan is only here for two days."

"Maybe you could embroider together or visit Widow Dorothy." Both were activities inside the walls of the city. It would make Damien feel better if she did not travel outside the walls.

"All good things, but I'm sure Megan would not be interested in them. She's young, Damien, going off to be married. I want to do something fun for her."

Damien sighed and sat back in the chair. "I'll go with you."

"Damien." Aurora captured his hand. "You must remain here and make plans to protect the borders of Acquitaine. To protect the castle." Anna began to braid her hair, moving one strand over the other.

Her people were always so important to her. Damien shook his head again.

"Please. For me. These are my people. I want them, as well as us, to be safe."

Damien looked at her. She had made up her mind. She was going on a picnic with her cousin. "Megan asked for a picnic, didn't she?"

Aurora grinned slightly.

She would do this to make her cousin happy, he knew. He shook his head. He understood but didn't like it. Finally, he sighed. "You will take a squadron of soldiers with you."

"Hardly a relaxed picnic."

"A *safe* picnic."

"Very well," she agreed. "For you, my love. I would like nothing more than to have a squadron of armed men following me to the Falls."

He leaned forward and kissed her lips. Every time he touched her, every time he kissed her, he loved her more. He was the luckiest man alive because she had chosen him.

Anna finished braiding her hair and tied the end with a golden bow. She stepped back, and Aurora stood. She took a glittering, transparent scarf from the table. "I will even wear the scarf you gave me."

Damien smiled at his sunshine. His love. His everything.

Adam, Justina and Gawyn were heading back to the room to pack to leave. Adam didn't understand why they had to leave. He loved it here! The falcons were amazing. And the knights. He wanted to be a knight! They were so brave.

Walking toward them down the hallway was Lady Aurora followed by a group of noble women. Behind them were a large group of soldiers.

Adam's heart melted when he spotted Lady Aurora. He loved her. She was so kind and so beautiful.

She smiled at them as they approached. "Good day, Adam. Justina. Captain Gawyn."

Adam noticed some of the women behind Aurora were carrying baskets. "Are you going on a picnic?" he wondered.

"Yes," Aurora answered. "We have a grand picnic planned. We're going to celebrate the marriage of my cousin."

A woman with golden hair stood at Aurora's side. Adam cast her a glance. She wasn't as pretty as Lady Aurora.

"Would you like to accompany us?" Aurora asked.

"Would I!" Adam exploded. He glanced back at Justina. A scowl furrowed his sister's brow and she shook her head. "Please," Adam begged. "Please, just this once. I won't ask for anything else. Please."

Justina's lips thinned in anger. Adam knew that look well enough to know the answer was no.

Adam frowned.

Aurora straightened. "Next time, Adam. It's all right." She led the group past Gawyn and Justina.

Adam watched her walk away. He clenched his jaw. He just wanted to go on a picnic with the princess. Was that too much to ask? Justina was so mean! He crossed his arms and gritted his teeth as they walked toward their room.

Gawyn stopped at their room. "Are you sure you won't stay?"

Justina didn't even look at him. She shook her head.

Adam knew that for whatever reason, Justina had made up her mind.

"I'll have your horse saddled. I'll wait for you in the inner ward." Gawyn walked away.

Justina opened the door.

Adam pushed by her into the room. "You're so mean. Why can't I go on the picnic?"

"Because it's time to leave."

"Why?" Adam demanded. "Why can't we stay?"

"It's not fair to leave Uncle Bruce alone with the all the chores."

"He said we could go! One more day. Please! I just want to go on the picnic."

Justina whirled on him. "And before that it was the falcons. What will it be next? Maybe you just want to move into the castle?"

Anger burned through Adam. He had never seen falcons before.

"Stop being so selfish. We are leaving."

Adam didn't move. He stood like a statue, glaring at his sister. He wanted to go to the picnic with the princess. She had invited him! And he would probably never be back here. Justina wouldn't allow it. He would probably never see Lady Aurora again because of his sister! He was going. He wasn't going to listen to his sister anymore. He ran to the door and threw it open.

"Adam!" Justina called.

"I hate you!" he snarled. He ran out of the room. He was going on the picnic and there wasn't anything she could do about it.

CHAPTER 9

$\mathfrak{J}$ustina raced out of the room. But Adam had reached the stairs already. She would never catch him, he was too fast. She sighed. Was she being too strict? He had never said he hated her before. The words had stunned and hurt her. She was furious with him for running, and disobeying her, but that couldn't override the feeling of anguish at his words. She sighed. Maybe just this one last time. Maybe she should let him go, there was nothing she could do about it now.

She returned to her room and sat on the edge of the bed for a long time. She debated what to do. She could wait here for Adam's return. Or she could... What? Do what? A strange need arose inside of her. An overwhelming need to see Gawyn, to let him comfort her. Just seeing him would allow her to reasonably go over her options, just talking to him.

Slowly, she made her way out of the castle into the inner ward. She spotted Gawyn almost immediately standing beside her brown and white horse. For a moment, her entire body wanted to be in the warmth and protection of his embrace. But she knew that was impossible. Still, she made her way to him.

"Where's Adam?" he asked.

Justina inhaled. "Apparently, he really wanted to go with Lady Aurora on the picnic."

Gawyn stared at her for a long moment. He drew himself up as understanding washed over him. "I'll bring him back."

Justina grabbed his arm. "No. No, let him go."

"Are you sure?"

Justina nodded. Of their own accord, her fingers moved through his. She wasn't certain if it was because she was hurt, or because she was confused, but it felt good when Gawyn squeezed her hand.

"You said no. He should listen to you."

"I know," Justina whispered. "But I'm not his mother."

Gawyn sighed softly. "Would you like to see more of the castle? I could show you the art gallery."

"What's that?"

"Lady Aurora's father collected some of the most remarkable art. It's stored in a long hallway."

Justina shook her head. "Just walk with me."

He nodded and signaled to the stable boy. "Keep the mare prepared. They will be leaving when the party returns from the picnic."

The stable boy nodded.

Gawyn looked at Justina. "Are you hungry?"

After the way she had acted toward him, he was still looking out for her welfare. "I'm sorry for the way I've treated you," Justina admitted.

He guided her over to the side of the wall where there was a wooden bench beneath one large tree beside the blacksmith shop. "I'm sorry for not being truthful."

Justina sat. It wasn't his fault. This entire mess. He was being truthful. It was time for her to do the same. "How well do you know Lord Damien?"

Gawyn hesitated. He had never been embarrassed of telling people Damien was his brother, but for some reason, his instincts told him not to tell Justina. "Very well."

Justina lifted her gaze to him. There was such sadness in her large brown eyes that he wanted to gather her to him and comfort her, but he didn't move.

Tears entered her eyes. "Did you know?"

"Know what?"

"What he was before he was Lord of Acquitaine."

Dread washed over Gawyn. He straightened and looked away from her. "Justina, I never intended --"

"Did you know?"

Gawyn hesitated. He could lie to her, but that would end badly. He sighed. "I know everything about Damien. He is my brother."

Her eyes widened in shock.

Gawyn grabbed her hands. "You have to understand -"

She pulled away from him. "Did you know what he was? Did you know he was a killer?"

Gawyn bowed his head, his eyebrows coming together in agony. "Yes," he whispered. "But that another lifetime ago."

She grabbed his tunic, desperately. "Did you know he killed my father?"

Gawyn startled, pulling back slightly. His gaze swept her anguished face. Slowly, understanding dawned. That was how she knew Damien. She had recognized him as the assassin of her father. "No. I didn't know every person he killed."

She pushed against his chest and stood. "But you knew he killed. You knew what he was, what he did."

Gawyn rose slowly, dangerously. "I knew. And it would be best for you to forget."

Justina gasped and her eyes teared. "Are you going to kill me if I don't?"

"Justina." Gawyn reached for her, but she pulled away violently. He stood for a moment with his hands outstretched before slowly lowering them. His heart twisted that she could even think he would harm her. "No." Gawyn watched the sadness creep over her, invade her body. He wanted to take her into his arms and comfort her, reassure her it had been a long time ago. That he and Damien were different men and they would never harm her. But she knew the men they had been. And he couldn't change his past. "Please, listen to me –"

"No, you listen! I saw him. I saw him standing over my father with a bloody dagger. He took my father from me! He must pay. He has to…" Her voice choked off and she whirled away.

Gawyn remembered the blood from some of his own kills. He knew the death. He would have sheltered her from all of it, if he could. If he had known her then. Still, the need to defend Damien was strong. "He's a good man now, Justina."

"A good man?" She turned back to him, her eyes ringed with unshed tears. "Is that why he sent you to kill me?"

Gawyn shook his head. "He didn't. I wasn't sent to kill you. I would never do that. We are different now." He looked away from her, understanding why she had to leave. It was better for her to be away from them.

"We?" she asked, shocked.

Gawyn realized his mistake too late. They could never be together. He was a fool to even think, to even hope… "I was an assassin, also."

Justina's mouth dropped open in shock. Her eyes twisted in contempt and her lips curled in disgust.

Gawyn had never seen the look. From Justina, it was like a sword plunged into his heart. "You wanted honesty." He reached his hands out in supplication. "I haven't done that since…since we arrived here." He shook his head fiercely. "I wouldn't…"

She pulled away from him as if his touch would burn her.

Slowly, Gawyn withdrew his hands. "I wanted you to know the truth. It's not just Damien."

Suddenly, a horse came charging into the inner ward. People scattered to get out of the way of the sharp hooves. Gawyn reacted instinctively and moved quickly into the path of the steed. He held his hands out above his head to stop it. It reared, and he had to step to the side before the hooves crashed down on his head. He seized the flapping reins, bringing the horse under control. It was spooked, or tired. He couldn't tell which.

The man on the horse was Sir Lewis, one of the soldiers who had rode with him to escort the Hungars to the borders. His hand clutched his side, his face a mask of agony. Gawyn handed the reins to the stable boy just as the soldier crumpled and slid from the saddle. Gawyn caught him before he hit the ground and eased him to the ground. He lifted the soldier's hand from his side to see blood pooling across his tunic. Gawyn looked around for help. One of the sentries was coming toward him. He pointed at him, ordering, "Get a physician."

The sentry whirled and raced away into the growing crowd.

Sir Lewis grabbed Gawyn's tunic, pulling him close. "The Hungars..." his voice trailed off as a coughing fit sprayed droplets of blood across Gawyn's tunic. "Rode around. Killed all the men. Burned the farm..."

Gawyn grimaced. He glanced at Justina to see the color drain from her face. Her uncle. He shouldn't have left them. "Where's Rupert?"

The soldier shook his head.

"How many?"

"Twenty-five. Fifty," he said. "They caught us off guard. We..."

"Take it easy, Lewis. Rest. Help will be here soon."

"All of them, dead."

"Rest. Don't talk," Gawyn ordered.

Blood bubbled from Lewis's lips. "They're coming. They're..." His hand went limp and slid from Gawyn's tunic. His eyes glassed over, and he stared, lifeless.

Gawyn straightened. The Hungars were coming. The castle was in jeopardy. He reached out to Lewis and closed his eyes before rising to his feet. There was work to be done. His mind churned. Damien needed to know. The people needed to be protected and the gates closed.

He looked toward Justina. The spot she had stood in was empty. He glanced around, at the bench they had sat on.

It was empty. His gaze moved over the courtyard, stopping briefly at the blacksmith shop and the door to the Keep. She was gone. He scanned the inner ward for her and caught a glimpse of her wild brown hair as she raced beneath the inner ward gate toward the outer ward. "Justina!" he called, but she didn't stop. He hurried after her, skirting guards, and peasants. He had to stop her. She couldn't leave the castle. It wasn't safe!

By the time he reached the gate, she was gone, swallowed up in a crowd of merchants and commoners. He stared into the outer ward, but there was no sign of her. He couldn't find her amidst the mass of people filling the outer ward. He cursed quietly.

One of the farms near the border had been burned, but he wasn't sure which one. It might be her uncle's farm. Justina wouldn't go there. He knew Justina was going to find Adam. Adam had gone with Aurora.

Aurora! He glanced back at the castle. He slammed a fist into the wall. He desperately wanted to pursue Justina and make sure she was safe. But he had responsibilities to the castle, the people of Acquitaine and his brother.

Gawyn hurried back to the inner ward. He glanced back at Lewis, satisfied to see the physician had arrived and was kneeling over him. He rushed to the sentry who had raced to get the physician. "Have the guards doubled. Raise the red flag and bring the villagers inside the walls."

The sentry nodded and hurried away.

Gawyn spun, looking over the sea of people again as if he would magically find Justina. But she wasn't there. She was gone, and he had a job to perform, responsibilities, duties to see to. The safety of the village and its people had to take precedence over one girl. He knew this, but it didn't help the crushing weight of guilt and worry that consumed him.

He had to find Damien. Gawyn raced into the keep. He ran through the hallways, dodging servants and merchants. He glanced in the Great Hall quickly, but Damien was not there. He took the spiral staircase two at a time and burst into the hallway. He ran past two nobles huddled in murmured talking to knock on Damien's door.

After a long moment, he pounded again. Finally, the door opened.

Aurora's lady's maid, Anna, greeted him with a slight bow.

"Where's Damien?" Gawyn demanded.

Anna pulled back slightly from his harsh tone. "I don't know. Perhaps the Great Hall?"

Gawyn didn't wait for anymore guesses. "If you see him, it is important I speak to him."

She curtseyed.

A tight knot formed in Gawyn's stomach. He wanted to go after Justina. He had to make sure she was safe. Yet, he had a dedication to his brother and to Acquitaine. Gawyn charged down the spiral stairway. It was the only time he wished the castle wasn't so big. As he reached the first floor and ran passed the Great Hall again, he saw a servant and grabbed his arm. "Where is Lord Damien?"

"I saw him heading toward the war room."

Gawyn spun and ran in that direction. He was wasting time looking for his brother. At least he had gotten word out to double the guard and bring the villagers inside. But it wasn't enough. It was hardly enough.

Finally, he spotted his brother entering the war room. It was so called because that was where they gathered to discuss matters of safety with the other constables at the castle. Gawyn should have known he would be there. If he wasn't so tired he would have known. It was the third day of the week and that was always what they did. Gawyn rushed into the room to see all the constables and lieutenants seated around a table. Gawyn knew them all. Damien was just taking his seat.

"It's the Hungars," Gawyn announced. "They've attacked a farm."

CHAPTER 10

Adam was out there and the Hungars were coming. It was the only thing Justina could think of. She had waited behind a merchant's cart until Gawyn disappeared into the Keep. He would try to stop her, and she wasn't going to stop looking for her brother. She wished she could have found a horse, but it didn't matter. She would find Adam. She *had* to find Adam.

Still, Gawyn's image came to mind as she hurried through the outer ward of the castle toward the portcullis. He knew what his brother had done, that he was a murderer. *He* was a murderer! Her heart broke. It didn't matter, she told herself firmly. She had to find Adam. Why didn't Adam listen to her? He could have been safe inside the castle. God, she hated the Lady Aurora for winning the hearts of men. For catching a young boy's eye.

She fought the surge of people moving into the castle and pushed forward over the drawbridge and into the clearing just before the castle. She crossed the clearing and reached the edge of the forest when a thunderous noise rose behind her. A huge group of mounted knights crossed the drawbridge. They headed away from the forest, away from her.

She wondered briefly where they were going. Where was she going? How did she know Adam was this way? She almost turned around and followed the soldiers. She *almost* did. But at the last moment, she continued in the direction she was heading.

All she knew was that Adam had to be safe. He was all she had left. She burst into the forest, running. Adam, her heart called. If he was the other way, the guards would find him. If he wasn't, she would find him. She *would* find him. She had to. A strangled gasp escaped her lips and she paused for a moment. What if she was too late? The image of her father lying in the street in a pool of blood came to her mind. No. No! She glanced over her shoulder. Through the trees, she could see the wall of the castle in the distance. Gawyn was there. Her entire being ached for him, ached for the comfort and security he offered, his love. She firmly pushed his dashing image from her mind to concentrate on Adam. He could help you, a small voice inside of her insisted. He is a killer, she answered. She would find Adam on her own.

A picnic. Where would they go for a picnic? She stopped. They had taken guards with them, surely the Acquitaine soldiers would be able to protect them from the Hungars. It would do her no good to panic. She had to remain calm. She continued moving forward, trusting her instincts, trusting what her father had taught her.

Aurora led the way through the forest. Bright sunlight shone through the leaves, creating a pattern on the forest floor. She was followed by her cousin, Megan, and the rest of the ladies, as well as the guards. She had decided to walk so they would not be far from the castle. She had even changed her mind about going to the Falls, the distant, beautiful water fall, and chosen McGregan Clearing. It wasn't as beautiful, but it was closer to the castle and an ideal place for a picnic. Damien would be proud of her for her wise choice.

They emerged into a clearing, bordered by trees on all sides. It was large and sunny.

"It's so beautiful," Megan said, reverently touching the glittering scarf.

Aurora turned and saw she was staring at the cloth Damien had given her. She removed the cloth from her neck and handed it to her. "Why don't you wear it today?"

"Oh no! Aurora, I couldn't!" Megan exclaimed, holding up her hands in denial.

"Please," Aurora said. "I insist."

"I'll tie it around your head," Lady Cathleen, one of the nobles accompanying them, said. She wore a beautiful green velvet dress and had her dark hair coiled up around her ears. She took the scarf.

Megan turned and presented her back to Lady Cathleen. Lady Cathleen tied the glimmering transparent scarf about Megan's golden locks.

Aurora watched as the other ladies cooed over Megan. She was enjoying Megan's happiness. She knew her cousin was anxious about her coming marriage. Not all women were as lucky as her to be able to pick the man they would marry.

Megan turned to her and threw her arms around her. "Thank you, Aurora!"

Aurora embraced her, holding her tightly. "It looks

lovely."

"Lady Aurora!"

Aurora turned to see the boy, Adam, racing toward her across the clearing. Her ladies giggled and whispered to each other. Aurora stepped toward the child, approaching him. "What are you doing here?"

Adam was out of breath but beaming with excitement. "You invited me to your picnic!"

"Your sister changed her mind?" Aurora asked hopefully.

Adam dipped his head. "Yes!"

There was something in the way he said it that she didn't believe. "Adam," she said softly. "Did she really change her mind?"

His shoulders drooped. "No." He looked up at her and his brown eyes filled with tears. "I'm sorry, Lady Aurora. I should have listened. But I wanted to come with you. I wanted --"

She lay a gentle hand on his shoulder while she glanced at her cousin. "Megan," she called. "Go and set up the picnic. The ladies will help you."

Megan turned and led the way into the clearing, her glittering scarf sparkling in the afternoon sun. The ladies followed her, the soldiers followed them at a discreet distance.

She didn't want the other women to see Adam's anguish. It wasn't right. She looked back at Adam. "What you did was wrong, you must know that."

"Aye," he said, sniffling, and rubbing his nose.

"Your sister must have had a very important reason for denying your attendance at the picnic."

He puffed out his lower lip. "She wanted to go

home."

"Then you should have listened to her."

Adam bobbed his head and his brow furrowed. "She's mad at me now," he whispered. "She probably never wants to see me again."

Aurora dropped to her knees before Adam, placing her hands on his shoulders. "That's not true. She loves you. She only wants what's best for you. Imagine how hard it must be on her. To take all that responsibility for you, and for her, on her own shoulders."

"I try to help her." Adam looked down at the ground.

"I know you do." She pulled Adam into her embrace, hugging him tightly. Poor child. He and his sister were arguing, and she wished she could do something to help the both of them, but Justina seemed not to want her help.

Suddenly, a large group of birds exploded from the trees on the other side of the clearing. Aurora turned her head. They rose like a black blanket into the sky. Silence settled across the clearing. The guards and the ladies had all paused and looked toward the birds.

One of the guards said something and motioned back toward the forest. No one moved at first.

Aurora rose slowly to her feet. Unease spread through her like a coming storm. The silence that spread through the clearing was eerie.

One of her ladies, Lady Elaine, took one step back toward the forest.

Horses exploded through the trees, racing across the clearing toward them. The men on the horses were screaming, swords raised in the air, reflecting sunlight in their polished silver. Their long hair rippled behind them, their bodies covered with animal pelts.

Hungars!

The guards drew their swords, but Aurora knew they would be no match for the men on horses. Some of her ladies screamed; all turned and ran toward the forest, leaving the picnic blankets and baskets on the ground. Lady Cathleen still carried one of the baskets as she ran toward the forest.

Aurora took a step toward them, her arms outstretched. Terror mingled with fear inside of her. The horses were going to reach them before they made it to the forest. Panic tightened in her chest. She signaled them to hurry with frantic waves of her arm. These women were her responsibility. Her friends. Her cousin. "Hurry!"

The horses charged across the clearing. One of the guards raced forward to intercept them, his sword held high.

The man on horseback barely slowed as he slashed his sword across the guard's throat. The guard spun in a circle, a plume of red spurting from his wound as he toppled to the ground.

Aurora gasped. The scene played out horrifically. She was stunned into immobility at the brutality.

The guards positioned themselves to protect the fleeing women as the horses thundered down on the them.

Shouts of excitement from the Hungars mingled with the screams of Aurora's ladies.

"Lady Aurora," Adam whispered, slipping his hand into hers.

She barely felt his tug, hypnotized by the graphic horror playing out before her. The horses trampled the soldiers as if they were nothing more than a row of flowers. Some of the guards fell; one horse reared and toppled to the side with a whinny.

Aurora stepped protectively in front of Adam.

"Run," she whispered to him.

Megan had picked up her blue velvet skirts and was running as fast as she could. She passed Lady Elaine.

One and then another guard fell trying to fight off the barbarians.

One of the horses closed on Lady Elaine. The barbarian leapt from his steed, knocking her to the ground. He stood over her for a moment, a wicked grin on his face. She screamed as he dropped on top of her, ripping at her dress.

Adam tugged on Aurora's arm. "This way."

"Run," Aurora whispered half in prayer, half statement. She watched her cousin run, the fear and desperation creased into the lines of her young face.

The leader's horse came up behind Megan and he swung his blade, hitting her in the back of the head. She fell, and he rounded his horse on her, sliding from the animal to approach her.

Aurora couldn't move, paralyzed with agonized fear. Megan! She jerked forward to go to her aid. But something was holding her back, pulling on her arm. Shocked and horrified, she looked down. Adam held her hand, tightly.

"We have to leave," he insisted, tugging her toward the forest.

Aurora looked back at the clearing.

One by one the Hungars reached her ladies. Screams echoed through the clearing, some filled with agony, some terror. One by one they fell.

Some of the guards were locked in combat with the Hungars; the clangs of their weapons mingled with the screams and echoed through the clearing. One of the guards slashed at one of the horse's legs as it galloped past him and the animal tumbled to the ground, head over heels.

Adam pulled hard on her arm. "Run," he said urgently.

She hesitated. How could she leave her people? How could she abandon them? How could she...? Damien. Damien! She had to reach him. She had to make sure he knew her people were in danger, that Acquitaine was under attack.

"Run!" Adam called.

Aurora turned. It was too late. A large Hungar stood behind her, his face twisted with hate.

Damien led the Acquitaine soldiers back into the castle, thundering across the drawbridge, through the outer ward and finally to the inner ward. His jaw was clenched, as were his fists. He dismounted without acknowledging little Joseph who took his horse's reins and rushed into the Keep. She had to be here. She had to... He burst into the Great Hall.

The servants looked up, startled.

Steward Thomas, a tall man with curly hair, immediately moved toward him.

Damien was halfway across the hall, calling, "Is she here? Did she come back?"

Steward Thomas stopped approaching and sadly shook his head. "No, m'lord. They have not returned."

Damien felt despair threatening to drag him into the darkness, but he refused to give up hope. He whirled to find the doorway lined with peasants and nobles alike, all staring. Their eyes were blank and lost. He hated them. Looking to him like he had the answers when he didn't give a damn about any of them.

Gawyn moved through the crowd and came toward him, but Damien brushed past him. Gawyn put a hand on his shoulder to stop him.

"I'm going to look for her," Damien growled. He jerked his shoulder away from his brother's hold. Nothing was going to stop him. He would find her.

Gawyn didn't let go, tightening his grip on Damien's shoulder. "Something came for you."

Damien looked at him. It was the first time he saw the apprehension and sadness in his brother's eyes. He felt an abyss opening around him and steadied himself. "Show me."

Gawyn dropped his hand and looked down. He nodded once. "In the judgement room."

Damien didn't hesitate. He moved out of the hall, past the people who congregated like vultures, waiting. They silently opened a path for him. He walked swiftly down the corridor. His senses heightened, the darkness inside of him shifting, waking. She had kept it at bay. He had always known it was still there, hiding from her light.

Damien threw the door open and entered. The room was empty and dark, only two torches flickered in the breeze from the doorway. He scanned the room. But there was nothing there. Nothing except for the chair Aurora sat in to give sentence. "Where?" he began, but then his gaze caught on something. Something golden and glittering. Every nerve froze. Every sense stopped functioning. No. He moved toward it like a statue, numb, cold, stiff. It lay on the chair where she had sat.

He stopped before the chair, staring. A bloody braid of golden sunshine wrapped in a sparkling scarf.

He was afraid to move. Afraid it might be real. He wanted so badly to blink and have it disappear. Her hair. He remembered seeing her that very morning with her hair braided. And the scarf. Maybe it wasn't the scarf. He reached out to touch it. His fingers brushed the material and it shifted. The sparkles reminded him of her eyes. That was why he had purchased it. Now, the glimmers were muted with smears of red. He pulled his fingers back to see the stain on his skin.

Her blood.

"Damien," Gawyn called softly from behind him. "It might not be hers." But his voice lacked conviction.

He knew the truth. Damien knew the truth. Tears blurred his vision. "Out," he said so softly that his voice barely escaped his lips. His life. His love. Aurora.

"Damien," Gawyn said more firmly. "You are Lord of Acquitaine. The people will look to you now. They --"

The darkness seized him, and he whirled on Gawyn. "GET OUT!" he hollered.

Gawyn stood immobile. Startled. Finally, he nodded and bowed slightly before retreating. He closed the door, sealing Damien in the tomb of death and darkness. Damien turned back to the braid. Complete and utter anguish swept over him in a wave of despair. His fists clenched. He didn't want to touch her hair. He didn't want to remember her this way. Had they tortured her? Raped her? In that brief second, it didn't matter. The only thing that mattered was that she was gone. And all that was left for him was darkness.

He dropped to his knees before the judgement chair. His chin fell to his chest. He couldn't protect her. He had failed. His gaze shifted to the braid in the chair. It couldn't be. It just couldn't be. She was everything to him. She was his life. She was his light. He felt himself swirling, falling into the dark, hopeless abyss. He threw his head back and a savage, anguished cry tore from the very depths of his soul.

CHAPTER 11

𝕵ustina worked her way through the forest, stepping over roots, ducking under branches. Her heart pounded in fear and dread. She had to find Adam. She wouldn't leave without him. She moved through some brush on the forest floor. The sunlight shone down between the leaves of the trees and Justina spotted a patch of white in the growth on the ground and paused. She carefully made her way toward it. The closer she came, the more she realized it wasn't Adam.

The white dress was long. A woman's form. Blonde hair. Not Adam. She almost moved away, but recognized Aurora's face. Shocked, horrified, she almost spun away to find Adam. If they had killed her, what had become of her brother?

A groan and then movement stalled Justina's movement.

Aurora rolled over, placing a hand to her head where a line of blood was trickling from a cut.

Justina dropped to her knees at her side, grabbing Aurora's shoulders and helping her to sit up.

Aurora winced in pain and looked at Justina with a

dazed expression.

"Where's Adam?" Justina asked, her fingers digging into Aurora's shoulders.

Slowly, as reality returned, a fearful look entered Aurora's stare. She looked about. "Run," she said softly.

Justina released her, looking around. Then, she leaned in close to her. "Where. Is. Adam?"

Aurora wobbled for a moment, then steadied herself with a hand to the ground. She shook her head. "He was here... and then..."

Justina shot to her feet and took a step toward the clearing.

Aurora seized her arm. "The Hungars killed everyone."

Justina tore her arm free. "He's my brother," she snarled with anguish and anger. She ran toward the clearing.

Aurora climbed to her feet unsteadily, but Justina didn't pause. She didn't care about the Hungars. She didn't care about Aurora. She had to find Adam. Frantically, she headed back. Her heart beat madly, desperately, fearfully. He had to be all right. He just had to. How could she have let him go? He was her responsibility. He was the last of her family. He was... everything to her.

She trudged through the growth on the forest floor, around trees, almost to the clearing. She spotted a dark form in the green of the forest floor ahead of her and her insides clenched in dread. She rushed up to the form, hoping it was a pile of dirt or logs. But as she stood over him, she recognized the brown tunic, the breeches, even the boots with the hole in the heel. He was on his stomach, his arms bent, his hands beneath him, his head turned away from her.

A ragged gasp escaped her as she dropped to her

knees beside him. "Adam?" She grabbed his shoulders and eased him onto his back. His eyes were wide and glazed, staring. His mouth was open in a silent cry.

I should have been here, Justina thought. "No," she whispered in a gasp. Her eyes scanned his small body.

His torso was covered in blood.

Justina lifted her hands to touch him, to somehow heal his wounds. But she didn't know where to start to make him better. She didn't know... She straightened, tears blurring her sight. "Get up, Adam," she commanded, her fingers squeezing his arm. "Get up. I told you not to go." Adam didn't rise. He didn't sit up. He wasn't listening.

Justina shook her head and dropped her chin to her chest. She felt moisture trail down her cheeks. Her lower lip trembled. "I told you not to..." She grabbed him and pulled him against her, pressing her cheek against his temple. "Adam. Don't go. I was supposed to take care of you." She hugged him fiercely, squeezing her eyes shut.

"Another girlie."

Justina opened her eyes. The world was blurred and unfocused through her tears. She heard someone moving behind her. She didn't want to let Adam go. Half of her didn't care if it was a Hungar. Half of her wanted to go with Adam. The other half wanted to kill every Hungar she could find. She pulled her dagger from the strap around her leg and slowly turned to face him.

A large, beefy man with long brown hair and ragged brown beard stood in the shadows of the trees. He wore the pelt of an animal across his huge shoulders. He looked her up and down and then laughed. "The boy had a little pig poker like that." He held up his hand. A small thin line of blood marred his palm. "Even cut me."

A whirlwind of rage swirled inside Justina. She didn't want to know what this barbarian had done to Adam. She rose to her feet, holding the dagger before her. "You did this?"

"I carved him up real good," the Hungar said with a grin. "Someone should have shown him how to use that poker."

"He's just a boy!" Justina hollered.

"A *stupid* boy. No one cuts me." He took a step toward her.

Rage, hatred, and an incredible sorrow overwhelmed her.

A thunk sounded from behind the Hungar and his head jerked forward. He grunted with the movement and lifted a hand to his head. He looked at his fingers which were stained with blood. He turned.

Aurora stood behind him holding a thick tree branch. She backed away, holding the branch before her.

He grabbed the branch and tore it from her hands, sending it flying away. Then he hit her with enough force to knock her to the ground.

Justina launched herself at him, jumping on his back. She ran the dagger across his neck, slicing deep. "My father taught *me* how to use this pig poker," she whispered into his ear.

He reached for her, but she leapt from his back. He whirled to her, blood gushing down the front of his stained tunic. He stumbled, grasping his throat, before toppling forward like a felled tree.

Justina stood over him, watching as the final throes of death shook his body. She felt a morbid satisfaction watching the life drain from him. Hate. It felt better that he was not taking a breath, that he was not wasting air by living.

But it didn't bring Adam back. Adam. She turned to her brother. He lay on his back; his arms open as if calling to her for a hug. She couldn't move. She couldn't go to him. The anger, the hate did not make him rise to his feet. It hadn't brought him back. She threw back her head, staring through the leaf dotted sky. Anguish consumed her, filling her body. She wanted to scream and shout and... cry. He wasn't coming back. Nothing could bring him back.

She was supposed to take care of him. Just like her father. She was supposed to take care of them. She should have watched Adam. Helped him. Disgust consumed her. She couldn't do it. She couldn't take care of Adam and she couldn't take care of her father. She couldn't protect them. An anguished cry bubbled in her throat.

A groan sounded from behind her. She whirled to see Aurora sitting up. Fury erupted inside of Justina. Her father's murderer's wife! How could she kiss the assassin? How could she bear to be near the killer? How could she love him? And yet, Adam had fallen beneath her spell, too. Contempt and loathing churned within her. Adam would never have been here if it wasn't for Lady Aurora!

Justina stepped toward Aurora. "I hate you!" Tears pooled in her eyes. "I hate you for being so beautiful. So kind. So...stupid!" She swiped a sleeve across her face. She signaled behind her at Adam with a swipe of her arm. "This is your fault." She lifted the dagger high above her head to end Aurora's life.

CHAPTER 12

Gawyn glanced down the hallway toward the large double doors leading to the inner courtyard. Two soldiers stood indecisively, staring at him as though he had the answers. Gawyn glanced at the door to the judgement room. Damien was in no condition to instruct the soldiers. He couldn't run a country. That had been Aurora's job. Aurora.

Gawyn's heart twisted for Damien. She had been kind and good and an amazing leader. And Damien had loved her.

Gawyn's mind wandered to another upstart of a girl. A beautiful girl. Justina was out there. She had gone after Adam, who was with Aurora. A sickening dread washed over him. If Aurora was...gone, where was Justina? He wanted to go and look for her. Surely, she was not with Adam. Surely, she had found her brother and made it to safety before the Hungars attacked.

Every instinct he had was telling him to look for her. He had to know she was unharmed.

Yet, his brother needed him. How could he leave him now? Good God! He was Captain of the guard. He had to do something. He marched down the hallway to the soldiers, only to turn the corner to find the hallway filled with concerned peasants and nobles and merchants. Gawyn hesitated.

Steward Thomas and Constable Grancourt, an older knight with graying hair and a stoic gaze, approached him.

"Captain, most of the village is inside the walls," Grancourt announced. "The gates are closed and secure."

Panic seized Gawyn's heart, clenching tight. How was Justina going to get back inside? He grabbed Thomas's arm. "Is Justina here?"

Thomas shook his head. "The little girl? The farmer's niece? No."

Gawyn pursed his lips. He was going after her. He glanced back at the judgement room door. "Keep those gates closed." That would keep Damien in the castle. His worst fear was that his brother would run off in some futile attempt to kill the Hungars for what they had done, knowing full well he would be killed. "Keep those walkways manned. I want every eye looking for the Hungars. They're coming."

At his proclamation, a murmuring of anxiety swept through the gathered group.

Gawyn glanced at the peasants and nobles a few feet from them, listening to every word. He seized Thomas's arm and put a hand on Grancourt's shoulder, leading them further down the hallway, out of listening range.

Gawyn looked at Grancourt. "Sir Grancourt, you are in charge until I return."

"Return? Where are you going?" Grancourt wondered.

Gawyn glared at Grancourt. "You are not to tell

anyone I am gone." He glanced at Thomas. "You either."

Both men nodded in understanding.

"Keep the walls manned. No one enters. No one leaves."

Grancourt bobbed his head. "Aye Captain."

"I'll be back as soon as I can."

Again, he nodded, but didn't ask where he was going.

Gawyn seized his arm in warrior fashion, clutching it just below the elbow, staring into his eyes. "The Hungars are out there. Don't let your guard down. Acquitaine must not be overtaken."

Grancourt nodded. "Aye, Captain."

When Gawyn released his arm with a firm nod, Grancourt hurried down the corridor, moving through the crowd of people.

Gawyn leaned close to Thomas. "Don't bother Damien."

"No, Captain," Thomas promised.

"Is there a way out of the castle, but not through the main gates?"

Thomas nodded. "The sally port."

Justina stood that way for a long moment, the dagger lifted high above her head, staring into Aurora's eyes. Shock and then fear passed in Aurora's wide blue eyes. Then she lifted her chin and Justina could have sworn she saw acceptance. Acceptance for what? Her death? Being so stupid! Justina wanted to kill her. She wanted to take her life for Adam. She wanted to drive the dagger into her heart, so her murdering husband would feel the same pain she felt when he took her father's life. Her hands trembled. She gritted her teeth.

Aurora bowed her head.

Justina let out a cry of frustration and lowered the hand holding the dagger. She couldn't do it. She couldn't kill her. Adam's death was not her fault. Her father's death was not her fault. Aurora was innocent, and she couldn't kill her.

Justina stalked away and then stalked back toward Aurora, pacing. Anger, anguish, sorrow all swirled inside of her. She wanted to sit on the ground and sob; she wanted to run and run and run; she wanted to scream. But she knew none of that would be enough. Not enough to right this. Not enough to bring her brother back. A numbing sadness swelled through her. She had no one left. She was alone. And then, one person suddenly came to her mind.

Gawyn. All she could think about was being held in his arms. She scowled. That was preposterous. Ridiculous! He couldn't make this right. But he could make this better. He could make her better. Tears entered her eyes and her shoulders slumped.

"I'm sorry."

Justina looked at Aurora. She knelt on the ground where she had been a moment ago. Justina couldn't say anything to her. Aurora had shown remarkable courage trying to bash the Hungar's skull in. The red mark on her chin was testament to that. And Justina had to admit she probably would not be standing there if Aurora hadn't done that. And that made her angry, too. She didn't want to be alive when her entire family was dead.

"I'm very sorry, but we should get back to the castle now."

Everyone Aurora had been with had been killed in the attack. Her ladies, the soldiers. She was hurting too. Justina clenched her jaw. The last thing she wanted to do was feel sympathy for her. Still, she had been kind to Adam. Justina shook her head as tears threatened to blind her again. She moved forward and grabbed Aurora's arm, pulling her to her feet.

Suddenly the snapping of a twig sounded, and she froze. She looked toward the sound but could only see dappled sunlight through the thick cover of the forest. As her gaze swept the forest, she saw the trampled dirt of the forest floor, footprints ground into the fallen leaves. So many footprints. She glanced at the ground beneath Aurora and all around her. The entire area was filled with footprints and trampled brush, almost as if an army had come through. Justina's grip tightened on Aurora's arm. An army of Hungars. "We have to get out of here."

Justina led her quickly away from the trampled forest. She paused to glance back at Adam. She couldn't think about him now. She couldn't. She would collapse into a pile of useless wailing. It wouldn't get them back to the castle. It wouldn't get her to Gawyn. Gawyn.

She was amazed at how she ached to see him, despite his profession of being a killer. A killer like his brother.

"This isn't the way to the castle."

Justina glanced over her shoulder at Aurora. Even through everything she had been through, she looked amazing. Her hair was braided and barely a strand was out of place. Her dress was not ripped. Justina couldn't imagine what *she* looked like. "No." She continued walking at a quick pace.

Aurora grabbed her arm, stopping her. "I have to

get back to the castle."

"The Hungars went that way. They are between us and the castle."

Aurora glanced toward the castle in horror.

"We'll have to find some other way."

"My people..."

"Will have to wait. If those Hungars find you..."

Aurora's face drained of color. She had seen what they would do.

Justina nodded. "We'll stay in the forest as long as we can. These are your lands. You know them. Is there somewhere we can go? Somewhere safe?"

Aurora looked at her and there was sadness in her eyes. "The waterfall."

"There's fresh water there?" Aurora nodded, and Justina continued, "I worry the Hungars would go there looking for water. Where else?"

Aurora looked down in thought. She opened her mouth and then closed it, scowling. "I thought my entire kingdom was safe. I just..."

Justina grabbed her shoulders. "We don't have time for doubt. The Hungars are out here. We have to find somewhere safe to hide."

Aurora shook her head. "I don't... I just..." Then her eyes lifted to meet Justina's. "Not far from the castle. There's a copse of trees surrounded by boulders."

"Boulders?"

"There are a lot of hiding places tucked in the boulders. The children like to play on them."

"How is that going to help us?"

"If we're lucky, they guards from the castle will be able to see us."

Gawyn was familiar with this path he steered his horse through. The path was on the way to McGregan Clearing, a favored picnic spot.

They had searched the waterfall earlier that day and found nothing. The only other spot Gawyn could think of for a picnic was McGregan Clearing. As the moon rose high in sky, Gawyn led his horse through forest path. When he heard talking in the distance, he tied his horse to a tree and continued on foot. He knew he couldn't leave Damien alone for long. He was out of his mind with remorse. He would do something foolish, Gawyn was sure.

But Gawyn had to search for Justina. He felt compelled to know she was safe. He had to find her. He would search around the clearing. Perhaps she was hiding with Adam in the forest somewhere. But why hadn't she returned to the castle? That's what worried him.

He would be lucky to find her, he knew. Especially if she were walking. It was unlikely they would bump into each other. The forest was too big. He walked further, keeping his eyes and ears open, scanning. Movement sounded to his left and he paused. But then he heard the scurrying of an animal. He relaxed slightly and continued forward. From tree to tree. He would stop, scan, and move. Until he saw an unnatural bump on the ground. The shape looked like a large person. Slowly, he drew a dagger from his belt. He waited, listening. Was it someone sleeping?

He inched forward. The man, it was obvious the rotund figure was a large man, did not move. The smell of blood was strong. When he stood over him, Gawyn saw the fur he wore across his large shoulders and recognized him as a Hungar. He glanced around to be sure there were no others. His gaze fell upon another dark form on the forest floor. Smaller. Much smaller.

Gawyn leaned close to the big man. No snoring. He leaned closer. No breathing. It took a moment to notice the ground beneath the man's head was slick with blood. He was dead. He pulled back to look at him. It was difficult to see anything but shadows in the dim night, but Gawyn made out a slash across the man's throat. His eyes narrowed slightly. Killed. By whom? Soldiers would inflict sword wounds.

Gawyn turned to the other form. He approached the small form. Before he got close, he could smell it. He had smelled death several times in his life and he would never get used to it. He stopped when he could see the outline of the small, thin body on the forest floor. A boy. His entire body clenched in dread. He didn't want to look, but he had to know. He bent beside the body, moving close to see his features. His eyes were open, staring off into the night sky. Gawyn recognized him immediately. Adam. He steeled himself against the agony that welled up inside him and shook his head in regret.

He whirled. Where was Justina? He circled the small area and couldn't find any more bodies. He stopped at Adam's side again. Had Adam killed the Hungar? No. Adam was too inexperienced to be of any threat to a warrior. It was probably the Hungar that killed Adam. Gawyn glanced back at the lump of a man. Then, who killed the Hungar? Someone had slit his throat.

A noise from the clearing beyond caught his attention. A rustling sound. He bent and stealthily followed the trampled leaves to the clearing. As he stepped from the trees, the moon broke through the clouds to shine down. Bodies lay scattered all through the clearing. The grasses were trampled around the corpses. Gawyn steeled himself and moved into the clearing. He walked to the first body. A woman. He gently turned her over. Lady Cathleen. Her eyes were wide, her lips parted in a silent scream.

Gawyn forced himself to be numb. He had seen death before. Even innocent death. But this, this was slaughter. An unnecessary killing. He clenched his free fist. Brutal. Women were no threat to armed soldiers. He slowly rose and looked around the clearing.

There were so many bodies and he would have to check every one, no matter how difficult it was. He had known these people, spent days with them. They were close friends of Aurora's. Aurora. Her body would be here, too. He forced emotion aside. At least he'd be able to return it to Damien for a proper burial.

He moved to the next body. He wasn't sure what he would do if he found Justina amidst the carnage. No matter what he did, he couldn't prepare himself for her death.

Once, darkness had been Damien's friend. Once, he had belonged to the shadows. But Aurora had come and banished them from his soul, revealing him as a hero. A good man. Now, he felt cold. Rage burned inside him, charring away the good man he had become. With Aurora gone, the beast lived again. He wanted blood. He wanted to kill the Hungars. Every last one of them.

Damien threw the rope over the wall, glancing one way and then the other. He knew he couldn't let the guards see him; they would never let him leave the castle alone. They would demand to accompany him. But this was something he had to do alone. He had been an assassin in another lifetime. He had been a killer. And he knew how to circumvent sentries and how to stay hidden. His instincts were heightened. He should have been amazed at how easily his past skills returned. But he wasn't.

The moon hid behind thick clouds as his feet hit the ground. He looked up the tall wall where the rope hung. His passage of return. If he made it. It didn't matter if he did or not. He would seek vengeance at all costs. He would be death's messenger. He snuck across the moat. He was an excellent swimmer and the dark waters held no peril for him. He came up on the other side and stayed low to the ground, moving along the moat until he saw them. The Hungar camp directly outside of the castle walls.

He clenched his teeth. Laughter floated around flickering fires and white tents. They had killed Aurora. They had killed his love. The words played over and over in his mind and his hands clenched so tightly that they shook. He wanted to kill them all. He wanted to make them pay for hurting her.

It would do no good to think of anything but his mission. There would be blood this night, he knew. The beast inside of him would be sated. He wanted the blood of one man. The leader. Hogar. The one who had given the order to take Aurora's life. To take her away from him.

He watched the camp, waiting patiently. Far too patiently for a man bent on death. He observed, taking in their laughter, their movements. Damien recognized the outline of Hogar, the big man with thick shoulders and arms. He crossed the campsite and disappeared into a tent.

Damien focused on the tent. He stayed low to the ground and moved toward the tent. He paused once when a shout went up from his left. A drunken Hungar stumbled onto one of the campfires while another laughed.

He froze until the scene settled down and the camp was quiet again. Then he moved quickly, quietly forward. Hiding behind a wagon, he scanned the area. From this vantage point, he was able to see the front of Hogar's tent. One guard. Hogar obviously thought there was no danger to him. The fool.

Damien slowly eased his dagger from his belt. No sound. No movement. Nothing. He would not miss this opportunity. Hogar would be dead before day break.

His hand shook with the image of Hogar lying in a pool of his own blood. Damien desired his death like he had no other.

He skirted the edges of the camp moving from shadow to shadow. The life of an assassin had returned, full force. It was almost as if he had never left it. It was different now. Such anger and the need for vengeance burned within him. He wanted blood. The beast inside him was demanding, hungry.

Inside Hogar's tent, he saw the leader move. He crossed the tent and lay down, leaning forward to blow out a tiny flame.

Damien waited. Patiently, anticipating. He paused, scanning to make sure no one was watching. He waited for what seemed like hours until he heard a snore issuing from the tent. He moved. He lifted the edge of the tent flap and crawled beneath the sheet, pausing halfway beneath to allow his eyes to adjust to the complete darkness.

Hogar slept on the ground like the animal he was.

Damien wasted no time. He moved swiftly, silently, deadly up to him until he stood over him. He placed the sharp edge of the dagger against his throat and moved his wrist.

CHAPTER 13

𝕵ustina led the way through the darkness, through the thick brush of the forest. She moved at a quick pace, the branches scratching her arms and face. Her dress caught in a bush and she ripped it free, tearing off some of the material. She didn't want to think. She just wanted to move. The faster she moved, the less she was able to think of her brother. She glanced back at Aurora. She was amazed that the noble woman was keeping up. "How much farther?"

"We have to cross a road and then maybe until daybreak."

She was breathing heavily, and Justina knew she was pushing her. Her gaze swept Aurora. Her hair was tight in the braid, her dress was untorn. She looked like she was refreshed and ready for a day in the Great Hall. "Do you always look so... amazing?"

Aurora looked down at her dress. "I do not look amazing."

Justina quirked her lips in disbelief. She turned to continue on.

"Do you have any other family members?"

Justina stopped cold. "Just my Uncle. But the guard said the farm had been burned." Silence spread through the forest and Justina clenched her jaw against the anguish that rose in her. She hadn't thought of Uncle Bruce until this very moment. "I don't think Uncle Bruce is alive."

"I'm so very sorry, Justina," Aurora whispered.

Justina shook her head and hardened her heart, pushing the sorrow down.

"If you had been at the farm, there's a good chance you would have been killed, too. I'm glad you were in Acquitaine."

Perhaps. But being in Acquitaine didn't save Adam. She wished she *had* been at the farm and she was dead.

"How did your mother die?"

"Mother died in childbirth with Adam. Your husband killed my father."

Crickets chirped in the distance, and the moon slipped back behind the clouds.

"That's why you looked at him the way you did at the square. The first time I saw you. You knew."

Justina couldn't answer. Yes, she knew. She knew he was a cold-blooded murderer. "He should be punished for the crimes he committed."

Aurora rose up like a lioness to defend him. "Why? He was ordered to commit those crimes. He was a slave and his master commanded him. Should he be punished for following orders?"

"Yes!" Justina snarled. "Do you know what it's like to have someone you love taken from you?"

Aurora lifted her chin. "I do. He killed my mother."

Shocked, Justina's mouth dropped open. "What?" She opened her mouth and then closed it. "How could you...?"

"I love him. He is not that killer anymore."

"He will always be that killer."

Aurora shook her head. "He is good and kind and a very wise ruler. He loves me. And I worry about him now. Alone, wondering where I am."

"Good. I'm glad he will be worrying. He should be worrying." She started forward again.

Aurora grabbed her arm. "Think on this, Justina. Damien is a dangerous man. But a good man. He will always do what is right."

Justina yanked her arm free of Aurora's hold. She didn't want to think on anything. Not Damien, not Aurora. Not Adam. She turned and moved on through the brush. Just Gawyn. And even Gawyn was dangerous. But her mind continued to search him out, to dwell on him. The way his eyes twinkled when he smiled, the way his hand engulfed hers.

Aurora called, "Do you hear that?"

Justina glanced back at her. She had her head cocked to the side, listening. "I don't hear anything."

"It sounded like flutes." Aurora began to make her way hurriedly through the forest.

"Wait! Where are you going?" Justina demanded. "It could be the Hungars."

"The Hungars do not listen to music. Not music like this." Aurora rushed through the brush with Justina following.

Justina grabbed her arm as they came to a road. "Wait." She pulled her down, so they knelt beside the road, behind a bush, and pressed her finger to her lips. She looked down the road one way and then the other. Toward the castle, she saw a small wagon and a campfire. She couldn't make out how many people were there, but she saw shadows moving. Then, again, the music started. Flutes playing soft tunes. A drum joined in and then clapping started.

Aurora leaned toward her to whisper, "Gypsies. They were at the castle to entertain us."

Justina was surprised there was no malice in her voice, only acceptance. Many didn't like gypsies, seeing them as thieves and whores. She wondered if they would recognize Aurora. That could be dangerous. What if they sold her to the Hungars? She was about to tell her they should continue, when a small voice came from behind them.

"I like yer dress." The voice was thickly accented.

Justina and Aurora turned to see a small girl standing amidst the brush beside the road. Justina was amazed the child had been so quiet, quiet enough to sneak up on them.

"Thank you," Aurora replied. She looked around the roadside. "Where's your mother?"

"At the camp," the girl answered. She shoved some beautifully thick black hair from her forehead. She wore a woolen skirt, tied around the waist with a black sash and a green tunic that was too big for her and fell off her shoulder. She squinted her eyes at Aurora.

"Where's your father?" Justina wondered.

"Papa is hunting in the woods."

Aurora straightened in dread. She looked at Justina and there was fear in her eyes. "We have to tell them."

"Tell us what?" The bushes parted, and a large man emerged. He was very tall and able, a bow and arrow slung over his shoulder.

Aurora stood immediately. "There are Hungars in the woods. You must be careful. They -"

127

Justina jumped up and seized her arm in a tight grip. "They were moving toward the castle."

He eyed them suspiciously.

Justina's hand dropped to the dagger in her belt.

"What are two women doing out alone in the woods at night?"

Cautiously, Justina answered, "We were trying to make it back to the castle, but we're cut off."

"Hmm." He eyed them again. Suddenly, a smile split his lips. "Then you must come back to camp and have some food!"

"We would, but we have to find a way into the castle."

"Pah!" He swept his arm out from side to side. "You cannot see in the dark. Wait until sunrise for your journey. I insist! I, Nicodemus, will see to your comfort this night!"

Justina swallowed her misgivings. What was she to do? She held Aurora's arm as they walked toward the camp. Run? She could run, but she wasn't sure how to convey that to Aurora. She followed with trepidation.

The small girl tugged on Nicodemus's pants leg. "I know her, Papa."

"I know, little one. I know."

Dread swirled up inside of Justina. He knew who Aurora was! He must have recognized her from the castle. This was not a good idea.

"Can you escort us to the castle?" Aurora asked.

"The drawbridge is raised. The gates are closed. You will not be able to enter until morning."

Aurora glanced down the road toward the castle anxiously. "They closed the gates?"

"Aye."

"Did all the people make it inside?"

"I do not know," his voice was strangely compassionate. "There were many, many people entering when we left."

"What were you hunting for out in the dark?" Justina asked.

He laughed. "I set traps! We need to eat. Rabbit. Mouse. I set the traps at night." He smacked his hands together, causing Justina and Aurora to jump. "And in the morning, we have food."

"You don't have enough food?" Aurora asked.

"We have enough for now because of the kindness of the lady of the castle, but others are not so kind to us. It is best to be prepared, eh?" Nicodemus laughed and picked the young girl up, tossing her above his head. She giggled as he caught her and set her on his shoulders. "Look!" Nicodemus called as they entered the camp. "Visitors!"

A small campfire illuminated the wagon. Two black horses were tethered to it. One woman set aside her tambourine to stand. She walked like a cat as she approached. Sleek, lethal. She circled them, eyeing them. "This little one is not worth much."

Justina straightened and scowled.

When the gypsy girl looked at Aurora, she gasped and glanced at Nicodemus.

"Be nice," he warned her. "This is Celina. There is Rolando." He pointed to the man near the drums with a thick mustache who stood up and bowed with a flourish, sweeping his hand out in front of him. "There is Terina." Terina sat on the steps of the wagon. She had wide eyes that seemed to see everything. "And he is Gerad." Gerad stood and approached them. He took Aurora's hand and looked deep into her eyes before bending over and pressing a kiss to her knuckles.

Justina almost groaned. Did everyone have to fall in love with her? But suddenly Gerad was before Justina. He captured her hand before she could yank it behind her back. "It is quite a pleasure." His smile was sensual, and his eyes were dark. He turned her hand over and pressed a kiss to her wrist. Justina blushed and pulled her hand from his hold. She wiped the kiss off on her skirt.

"We must get back to the castle," Aurora said. She glanced at Nicodemus. "When can you take us to the castle?"

"There is no hurry," Gerad said in his heavily accented voice. "Surely, you can share a meal with us before you go."

Aurora glanced at Justina.

"There are Hungars in the forest. You should be on your way. *We* should be on our way," Justina warned.

"Oh, the Hungars!" Rolando called. He pounded on one of the drums. "They are large and not very bright."

"But they have sharp swords."

Nicodemus nodded, scooping the girl from his shoulders, and setting her on the ground. "Aye. And they are certainly no lovers of music."

Justina glanced toward the castle.

"Come!" Nicodemus called, leading them into the camp. He slapped Rolando on the back of the head. "Get up! Give your seat to our guests!"

"We don't mean to be disrespectful, but we have to get to the castle," Aurora insisted.

"As I said, the gates are closed and the Hungars roam the forest. It is a dangerous time. The morning would be better to travel," Nicodemus replied.

Aurora scowled deeply.

"Here! Drink. You must be thirsty!"

Justina realized she was thirsty, but she wasn't sure she trusted these gypsies enough to drink what they had.

The little girl raced into the wagon and when she emerged again, she was holding a flask. She handed it to Nicodemus. He handed it to Aurora. "It is not quite what we tasted at the castle, but it satisfies our thirst."

Aurora shook her head and waved it away.

"I insist. You must drink for your journey," Nicodemus said, offering the flask again.

Aurora took the flask, opened it and took a quick drink. She handed the flask to Justina.

Justina eyed it wearily. But in the end, her dry throat won out and she took a deep drink. "You haven't seen any Hungars?"

"No. The Hungars are not very friendly with our kind."

Celina leaned up against Nicodemus. "They would have been very friendly to me, eh?"

Justina sat on the stump vacated by Rolando.

Aurora looked back at the castle. Then turned to Nicodemus. "Can we borrow one of your horses?"

Nicodemus smiled patiently. "It is not wise to travel at night. Besides, the horse's steps would attract unwanted attention."

The little girl stood at Aurora's side, staring up at her with wide brown eyes.

Brown eyes that reminded Justina of Adam. A lump rose in her throat and she shot to her feet. They couldn't stay here! They had to keep moving. "We should go."

"Go?" Nicodemus echoed. "Where would you go? It is dark and not safe for two women to be traveling alone. Eat with us. Rest. We will play music for you and we will dance."

Aurora met Justina's gaze. Desperation filled her wide eyes.

"We will escort you to the castle in the morning," Nicodemus promised. "For now, let us keep you safe."

Celina started jingling the tambourine. Rolando began to tap the drums in a rhythmic sound.

Nicodemus took Justina's hand gently, carefully and led her to the center of the camp. He began to move his hips, swaying from side to side and stomping his feet. "Come, girl. Dance."

But Justina could only stand as tears rushed to her eyes. How could she dance when Adam was gone? How could she be happy? She shook her head.

Gerad stood from the spit, staring down the road. "A rider."

"Here," Nicodemus called, indicating the shadows of the wagon with a wave of his hand. "Behind the wagon. You must remain hidden."

CHAPTER 14

Gawyn spurred his horse hard toward the gypsy camp he had spotted on the road. Justina! She might have sought protection with them. Or perchance they had seen her. He needed to find her. Desperation was rising in him and he had to push it down time and again. Too many images rose in his mind's eye. Justina lying wounded in a patch of grass. Had he missed her? Doubt festered. Justina's clothing torn and her legs spread.

He tightened his grip on the reins of the horse, and it came to a halt, rearing slightly.

The large man approached him.

Gawyn recalled seeing him in the castle during the judgements.

"Greetings!" he called. "You ride late at night, my friend. What brings you out in the dark?"

"I'm looking for a woman," Gawyn told him.

"Aren't we all?" Nicodemus roared in a hearty laughing voice.

"Her name is Justina. I have to find her. She has dark hair and is wearing --"

"Gawyn," a voice whispered.

Gawyn turned. For a moment, he thought it was a dream. She stood there, beside the wagon looking breathless. His heart missed a beat at the sight of her. "Justina," he whispered. His voice was ragged as if her name had been ripped from the depths of his soul. He realized he had been preparing himself for her death. He slid from his horse and rushed forward. She met him halfway, throwing her arms around him. He caught her, and she slumped in his arms. He physically held her up, supporting her. He couldn't resist pressing his lips to hers with such relief and elation that his knees almost buckled.

Her face was moist and hitching sobs came from her open mouth.

Gawyn pulled back to look into her red eyes. Her long, dark lashes were clumped together. He looked down at her face, framing it with his hands. He stroked her cheeks with his thumbs, trying to wipe her agony away, yet knowing he could never do it. Just looking at her sent waves of desperation and relief and an explosive need through him. He pulled her tight against him, holding her.

She pressed her wet face into his chest. "Adam..."

"I know," he whispered, stroking her hair.

Around them, the gypsy camp was strangely quiet. Gawyn scanned the area over her shoulder. They had to get out of there before Hungars tracked them. They weren't safe here. He tucked her protectively beneath his arm and turned.

Aurora stepped from the bushes beside the wagon. She stood absolutely still for a long moment.

Gawyn blinked. It was as if she had materialized from the darkness. "Aurora," he called in relief and held out the arm that wasn't holding Justina for her.

Aurora came forward into his embrace.

He squeezed her tightly, desperately glad to see her. "Damien thinks... we all thought you were dead."

Aurora shook her head as she pulled back to look at him. "It was Megan. They --"

"Never mind," Gawyn interrupted quickly. She didn't need to relive the horror he had seen in the clearing. It must have been Megan's body he had seen and mistaken for Aurora. They had bashed in her face beyond recognition. "Damien thinks you're dead. We have to get back to the castle."

The lead gypsy took a deep breath. "Two sobbing women. I don't envy you, my friend."

"Thank you for taking care of them," Gawyn said. He released Aurora but kept Justina close to him. They all began toward his horse.

Aurora stopped and turned to the group of gypsies. "You were kind to us. You are welcomed back to Acquitaine as honored guests anytime."

The man took her hand and pressed a kiss to her knuckles. "We were only returning the favor, my lady."

They barely said anything as they made their way back toward the sally port. Aurora rode the horse, but Justina refused and Gawyn kept her in his hold. Both women looked ragged and tired. He continued to look down at Justina as they walked. There was a sadness in her eyes he knew he could never erase. Her father, her brother, gone. It seemed like every time she came near Damien, someone died. Although it had not been his fault. If only Damien had not wanted him to find out what she knew. If only she had not caught his brother's eye, she would have lived on the farm, peacefully. But then, he never would have met her. He pressed a kiss to her forehead and it drew her attention. She met his gaze and tightened her hold around his waist as if she thought he would vanish.

Gawyn looked at Aurora. Her chin was falling to her chest.

Gawyn glanced toward the castle. The wall surrounding the city was in the distance, a target within striking distance. They would make it there by sun up. It was slow going having to walk, but three would not fit on the horse. "Let's rest here." Gawyn began to lead the horse off the path.

"No!" Aurora cried. "We can't."

"Aurora, you're exhausted. Just a short rest and we'll be on the way. I promise we won't be long."

Aurora glanced down at Justina. She gently bit her lower lip and consented with a nod.

Gawyn knew she was concerned about Damien. As was he. But he had to be realistic. Both Justina and Aurora had been up all night. They had experienced horrendous death. It was a man's world to deal with that type of violence. A woman had no place in it. And he wanted to shelter Justina. He had wanted to, but he had failed.

When they reached a small stream, Gawyn lifted his arm from Justina and helped Aurora dismount. Then he led the horse to the stream, allowing him to drink. He wished he had a flask of ale for the women, but he had ridden out of the castle without any provisions, intent on finding Justina. His gaze swept her. She stared at the ground, her long dark hair hung in waves past her slumping shoulders. Her brown dress was stained with smears of blood. She knew about Adam. Had she been there? It didn't matter. The only thing that mattered was that she was safe. His gaze moved to Aurora who was staring at the castle. And Aurora...

He was glad she was alive. Very glad.

"We'll make our way to the sally port. Steward Thomas is waiting there." He touched Aurora's arm. "Don't worry. We'll be home soon." She glanced at him and nodded, but there was no belief in her eyes.

"Are the gates closed?" she asked.

Gawyn nodded. "When I left, the castle was sealed. The Hungars had not attacked, but we knew they were out there."

She looked back at the wall. "Because we didn't return."

"Lewis made it back from Auch and told us the Hungars attacked. Aurora, we went to the falls looking for you."

She nodded again. "I decided to go to the McGregan Clearing. It was closer to the castle. Safer, I thought."

He grabbed her arms and turned her to face him. "You didn't know. How could you? This is not your fault."

"I am of lady of the castle." Tears entered her blue eyes. "I made the choice to picnic there."

"And on any other day, it would have been fine. A perfect day to frolic in the grass. You had guards with you."

"My ladies... All of them... My cousin." Her voice broke.

"Aurora," Gawyn said firmly, his fingers gripping her arms tightly. "Your people need you now. Damien needs you."

She looked back at the wall, as if she could see him

and blinked away her tears. When she finally spoke, her voice held conviction and authority. "Then why did we stop?"

Gawyn smiled in satisfaction. "We'll leave in a moment." He turned to Justina. She was watching them with weary eyes. Her lips turned down at the corners. He knew she was tired, but also knew her lower lip trembled from sadness. He moved over to her and lifted her chin with his finger. "Are you okay?"

She sighed. "No. But I'll make it to the castle."

He couldn't resist brushing a strand of her hair from her cheek and letting his fingers linger against her skin. When he knew she had gone after Adam, risking her own life, some part of him went mad with worry. But, she was safe. "I wish I could have saved him."

Justina shook her head. "I know. You would have if you were there. But you weren't."

He took her hands and kissed each one. "I'm sorry."

She wrapped her arms around him and he squeezed her tightly, holding her, comforting her as best he could. She buried her face against his shoulder.

"Gawyn," Aurora called. "What's that?" She pointed off to the distance toward the castle.

Gawyn joined her. Just before the castle, in the clearing to the right, there was a glimmering light that grew brighter as he watched. It could be nothing other than a fire. As they watched, another joined. Dread and apprehension filled Gawyn. "It's the Hungars. Time to go." He lifted Aurora onto the saddle. He turned to Justina. "Sorry, but we have to hurry. You must ride."

She opened her mouth to protest, but he lifted her and settled her behind Aurora. His gaze shifted to the flames. Campfires. They were laying siege to the castle. He took the reins of the horse and began to jog toward the castle.

The problem was they were very close to the sally port. Very close.

CHAPTER 15

Gawyn jogged beside the horse, keeping a watchful gaze toward the sally port. He purposefully went to the other side of the castle, trying to remain under the cover of the trees. The sun was rising behind him and he knew this wasn't a good thing. His cover would be gone. He paused just before the wide clearing that stretched before them. If they could make it across the clearing and the moat that surrounded the city wall, only the massive wall of the city stood in their way. It didn't look good. One obstacle at a time.

Gawyn was breathing heavily, but he never stopped scanning the area, looking for Hungars or a way into the village. The large wall was all encompassing, circling the village. The moat ran in a semicircle around the city wall, connecting to Sterling river in two spots. "Aurora, do you know how the castle gets its water?"

"There is a well in the center of the village and another inside the castle," she answered.

He nodded. "Does the water come from the river?"

She looked at the river. "I suppose it does. I don't really know for sure."

Gawyn scanned the tops of the wall but could see no guards. He assumed the Hungars had not breached the village wall. Why would they camp outside of it if they had? Most of the guards would be on the other side of the city wall, defending it from the Hungars. They were on their own.

He glanced at Justina on the horse. She stared at the wall with concern. He was never going to leave her again. The women would come with him. He just hoped there was some way to gain entrance to the village.

He moved through the forest, trying to put distance between the Hungars camp and them. He went as far as he could in the forest, until he came to Sterling River. He looked toward the Hungars camp, but the city wall blocked his view. He tethered his steed to a tree, hoping to return for it. He reached for Justina and helped her from his horse. Then he helped Aurora dismount. "We walk from here. Try to stay low." He took Justina's hand and glanced toward the other side of the wall, toward the Hungars camp. It was hidden behind the wall. He hoped that would give them a measure of safety as they raced across the clearing.

He looked up at the sky. The grey of night was fading to be replaced with pinks as the sun began to climb higher. They had to go now. He was hoping the wall would keep them hidden from the Hungar's view. This was so risky. If it were only him alone...

He took a deep breath and started across the clearing toward the wall. He kept a watchful eye on the other side of the wall, fearful a horde of Hungars would come charging toward them. He pulled Justina on, refusing to release her hand. He wasn't going to lose her again. Not after the panicked anguish he had felt. He would die first. The thought startled him. He quickly pushed it aside. He would think of it later. He cast a glance at Aurora who was right behind them. She held her skirt up so as not to trip on it, but she was doing as he said, ducking her head and racing after them.

A mad dash toward the wall. Crazy. Insane. Because he didn't even know if it would offer them safety or entry. He couldn't think of any other way in. He knew the layout of the castle and the city but had never had to get inside. His thinking had always been to keep others out.

They came to a halt at the moat. Gawyn led them as close to the river as he could for protection, out of eyesight of whatever Hungar sentry might come this way. They were still vulnerable out in the open. They would have to cross the moat to get to the wall. He tugged Justina forward. She resisted, and he glanced back at her. She was staring at the water. "It's all right," he whispered. "I'm right here."

"How deep is it?" Justina asked, her gaze on the slowly moving moat.

Gawyn looked at the moat. He saw logs floating together, suspended in the dark water, but he couldn't see the bottom. "I don't know."

"I'll go," Aurora offered. She stepped forward.

Gawyn caught her arm. "Can you swim?"

Aurora nodded. She moved into the water slowly. Gawyn stepped closer until his boots were in the water. He felt guilty having her go first. He should have been the one to test the waters.

She paused and shivered. She looked at the wall of the city and lifted her chin and straightened her shoulders before moving into the black water. The dark liquid moved up her legs the further she got until she was waist deep.

Gawyn took another step forward without relinquishing Justina's hand. His gaze locked on Aurora as she moved through the water. He was ready to dive in, if she needed him. Halfway through the moat, she lurched forward, swimming.

"No," Justina murmured, pulling her hand from Gawyn's hold. "I can't."

Gawyn waited, watching until Aurora got her footing on the other side of the moat and walked out of the water. He nodded to her and turned to Justina.

Justina's gaze was locked on the water, her eyes wide with fear.

Gawyn eased her chin up until her gaze met his. "Look at me."

"I can't swim," she whispered. "The water is over my head."

"You don't have to," Gawyn said softly. "Just hold onto me. I won't let anything happen to you."

"I'll wait here. I'll be fine." Her gaze darted to the top of the wall. "I'm so close to the wall. I can just wait here." She nodded, satisfied with her plan. As her gaze settled on Gawyn's she winced.

Gawyn's gaze moved slowly over her face, his lips twisted in a humorless grin. He was not going to let her wait here.

She shook her head. "I can't."

He took her hand and began to lead her into the water. A step. Then another. He held her hand tightly.

She stopped walking as the water soaked her slippers and the hem of her skirt. "I can't, Gawyn."

"You have to," he insisted. He took both of her hands into his own.

She shook her head, her eyes wide. "I can't do it. Adam was the swimmer. I never could."

Gawyn's gaze swept her face with compassion. Her brown eyes shifting between him and the water at her feet. Her forehead wrinkled with concern. She had been through so much. He would not force her. He nodded. "Then we'll wait here. Maybe someone will see us from the walls before the Hungars find us."

"No." She pulled her hands from his hold. "You go. Aurora needs to lead her people. She has to get into the castle."

"I'm not leaving you." It was a statement. He wasn't going to leave her. Not now. Not ever.

Justina glanced at the water. Conflict swirled in the depths of her eyes. "You have to go, Gawyn."

"I lost you once and I am not going through that again."

Sympathy washed over her, and she shook her head, looking down. She pulled her hand from his. "Fine," she growled. She stomped into the water another foot and stopped as it lapped at her knees. "I'll drown then."

He smiled warmly at her courage. "I won't let you drown. You can hold onto me." Again, he took her hand and tucked it beneath his arm. They moved deeper into the water. He felt Justina's resistance, her stiffness and hesitancy, but she moved with him. "You can lock your arms around my shoulders. I'll hold onto your wrist as I swim."

"You know how to swim."

They were waist deep in the water now. "I'm a very good swimmer," Gawyn said softly. He continued forward, talking to her. "Your feet won't touch the ground, but mine will. For a bit."

Justina glanced across the water to the other side where Aurora stood near the edge, waiting for them. She grumbled. "Does she have to do everything perfectly?"

Gawyn chuckled a rich, throaty laugh. "I'm afraid she does."

Justina stopped moving as the water lapped at her chest. She was breathing quickly, eyeing the liquid around her with trepidation and fear.

"Are you ready?"

"No."

Gawyn presented her with his back. His grip moved to her wrist. "Under my arms, clasp your hands around me by my chest. Lock them in front." He leaned back slightly so she could do as he told her.

"Anything to get me to hug you," she whispered.

Gawyn could hear the tension in her voice. He pulled her against him. She reached around him with her other hand and locked hands tightly at his chest as if she were praying.

Gawyn straightened and she was on the tips of her toes. He pressed her arm against his chest. "Remember, I'll be on my feet. You'll be floating for a little. Ready?"

"Don't let go."

He looked over his shoulder at her. Terror ringed her large brown eyes. "Never," he vowed. Then he moved forward as quickly as he could before she could change her mind. The water was up to his neck. "Just keep your head above water." He launched himself forward and swam with one arm. He tried to keep her on his back, as he swam with one arm and kicks of his feet. He still held her arm against him. He was a strong swimmer and continued forward with strokes and kicks. Finally, his feet touched the ground and he walked forward until she was able to get her footing. Still, she didn't release him for a long moment as he moved toward dry land. He looked back at her with a proud grin. But she rushed by him until her feet were on the dry earth.

"Don't ever make me do that again," she told him.

Gawyn nodded but made no such vow. He knew it might get worse. There was no entrance to the castle on this side. No sally port. He had hoped to find an underwater entrance. Somewhere the river entered the castle to get to the wells. But now, he doubted even that. The only other option was to try to move through the river to the other side and try to sneak to the sally port. Either way would be dangerous. Either way would require Justina to get in the water again. He moved over to where the river met the land of the castle, searching.

"Gawyn," Aurora called.

Gawyn looked back at her. She was pointing to the side of the wall. Hanging from the wall was their salvation. A long piece of rope, barely visible by the naked eye. Gawyn began to smile.

CHAPTER 16

Damien sat in the judgement room. It was dark, but his eyes had adjusted, as had his body. He knelt before Aurora's braid, his head hanging down, his chin against his chest. The beast was alive in him now, demanding more blood. Demanding revenge. He knew he had scared the servants enough, so they would not bother him anymore. He didn't care. He didn't care about them. He didn't care about Acquitaine. She was gone. His light was gone.

He heard the door creak open behind him. His jaw clenched tight.

"Damien?"

Gawyn. He had wondered where his brother had gotten to. He wondered why he wasn't there, trying to comfort him. He needed no comfort. Only death. "Get out," he whispered. It was so silent that his voice echoed through the room.

Gawyn didn't seem to notice. A torch flared to light behind Damien. He scowled at the light on the floor as if the touch of it would burn him.

"Have you eaten anything?"

Always intrusive. Damien's fists clenched tight. He wanted him gone. He wanted to be in darkness. He wanted to be cold and alone. She was gone. Some part deep inside of him was wailing and he couldn't get it to stop unless he saw red. "Get out," Damien said more firmly. The beast was hungry. Damien snarled, his lips curling over his teeth.

"Brother," Gawyn began with a gentleness.

Damien whirled, his hands curved into clawed fists, his rage blinding him, his teeth bared. "GET OUT!"

Gawyn stood, holding a torch. He didn't flinch at Damien's tirade, he didn't move.

The torchlight showered over her like beams of gold touching a goddess. For a moment, Damien froze. He didn't even take a breath. He must be going mad. Slowly, his hands uncurled. His snarl evaporated. The beast howled inside of him, telling him to run, to hide. She couldn't be real. He was going mad.

She came toward him. But it wasn't until he heard her voice, a soft calling, "Damien," that he knew this was no dream, this was no hallucination.

He was at her side in two large strides. Tears welled inside of him as he stopped before her, his gaze hungrily devouring her every curve, every line on her face.

She touched his cheek, her stroke gentle, concerned.

Fiercely, savagely, he grabbed her and pulled her to him, holding her, crushing her to him. He squeezed his eyes closed, afraid so afraid that he would open them, and she would be gone. A lone tear squeezed from the corner of his eye, running over his cheek.

"Damien, Damien," she whispered over and over.

Her voice was the only thing anchoring him to the moment. And still he crushed her to him, refusing to relinquish her softness, her goodness. Her love.

When he heard a soft sob, he pulled back to look at her. Her face was wet with tears. He ran his thumbs over her cheeks, brushing them away. She was safe. He kissed her lips, tasting her. She was real.

The door creaking drew Damien's attention. He saw Gawyn pause for a moment in the doorway. They locked eyes. He had brought her back to him. His brother had brought her back.

Justina sat in her chambers; Gawyn was seated at the table, watching her. They were still in the wet, muddy clothing they had crossed the river in even though a tub of warm water had been brought in and was set before the hearth. She jumped up from her bed and moved to the window. She stared out at the sun. Midday. She was feeling restless and lost.

"Are you hungry?"

Justina turned to look at him. "I want him back."

Gawyn stood. "Justina --"

"I mean I want to bring him home to bury him. He shouldn't be out there alone."

Gawyn nodded. "I know. But, we can't go now."

Justina turned to look at him. Their clothing was damp, but at least the hearth was lit for warmth. He had carried her up the wall on his back, using the rope and then had done the same for Aurora. He must have left the castle to look for Aurora. She was more important. She dropped her head and turned away to look out the window again.

"What is it?"

"You saved my life."

He said nothing.

"I suppose you rode out looking for Aurora and I --"

"We had just gotten back from looking for her. I should have stayed with Damien. But the only thing I could think of the entire time was the fact that you had rushed out of the castle to search for your brother." She turned to look at him. "You were out there alone."

Justina looked down, half shrugging, half nodding. "It was foolish. I know. But I had to know. I had to find him."

"As did I."

Justina peered up at him. "You had to find Aurora."

"I had to find *you*."

"I don't understand."

"Neither do I. But the moment I found you safe with the gypsies..." He shook his head and ran his hand through his hair. "It was like... like..."

"Like a ton of mortar stones had been lifted from your shoulders. And that maybe there was hope. Maybe everything was going to be all right." It was how she felt the moment she had laid eyes on him. She couldn't help it. She lifted a hand and touched his cheek. "Thank you for looking for me."

He wrapped his arms around her, drawing her close against him.

He was so hard and so strong. She had been so wrapped up with protecting her brother and being responsible for him that she failed to see how much Gawyn had come to mean to her. Even though...

She stepped back, bowing her head.

"What is it?"

"I know what you were. I know that you killed people. But when I was out there, it didn't matter. I only thought of you."

Gawyn nodded but made no move to come to her.

"You knew how I felt and you still came for me."

"I had to."

"Why?" Justina asked. Gawyn looked at her with such tenderness and such longing that Justina's heart melted.

"I've never felt this way about anyone. You've surprised me at every turn. No one does that." He took a step closer to her. "You are all I think about. All I desire." He traced a curl of her dark hair. "I think I just might be falling in love with you."

"Me?"

He took a step back from her, dropping his hands to his side. "I'm so sorry I let you down, Justina. And I would understand if you never wanted to see me aga—"

She entwined her hands around his neck and lifted up on her toes to press her lips against his. Let her down? He never let her down! He had come after her, knowing the Hungars were attacking! He loved her! Her heart sped up and her pulse quickened in response to his closeness, to his touch. She parted her lips for his exploration. His kiss was surprisingly gentle and patient. She trembled at the sweet tenderness of his touch. But it wasn't enough for her. She wanted to lose herself in him. She wanted to love him.

She stepped back toward the bed without breaking the kiss, pulling him with her.

He hesitated. "Justina," he said softly.

"Please Gawyn. Please. Don't deny me. Not now."

"Are you sure?" he asked. "You've been through so much."

Always thinking of her. What more could she ask? "I think we should get out of these dirty clothing." She ran her hands over his strong shoulders.

Gawyn acquiesced with a nod. He pulled her over to the steaming tub. He picked up a towel, dipping it into the water. He ran the cloth over her forehead, the dirt coming off her skin. He dipped it in the water again and brushed it across her cheeks and her nose, then her chin, cleaning her face. He grinned. "I can't imagine how I look."

Her gaze swept his face. His strong nose, sensual lips and warm brown eyes. "Amazing," she whispered.

He smiled, and some caked dirt fell from his cheek. His gaze swept her and everywhere his smoldering look touched, prickles of heat flared to life. He took hold of her floor length tunic and paused. He looked her in the eyes as he slowly lifted the garment over her head. Pieces of dried mud fell off the tunic to the floor. She stood in her chemise.

The warm fire crackled in the hearth behind her.

Gawyn lifted his tunic over his head, revealing his glorious torso inch by inch. He was magnificent. A fighter. Hard planes lined his ridged stomach. The muscles of his upper body were defined and sculpted. He was much stronger than she had believed. She eased the cloth from his hand and dipped it in the water. She brushed the cloth across his shoulders and drops of water fell over his skin. She slowly slid the cloth across his chest and his dark nipples tightened. The dirt came away leaving a gleaming, glowing torso.

Justina stared at his magnificence. She wanted to see all of him. She untied his leggings, but Gawyn caught her hands. He stepped back and pulled one boot off and then the other. Both landed on the floor.

He returned to her side and Justina eased his

leggings down. She reached behind him to push them over his bottom, letting her hand slide over his skin. Warm, soft. When she pulled back, she saw just how excited he was. She lifted her gaze to his face again.

They came together in a rush of longing and need. Their bodies fusing, their kiss desperate and heated.

They made love in the tub and throughout the night. Spending their time in each other's arms, forgetting the world for just one magical night.

In the morning, Gawyn donned clean clothing and pulled his boots on.

Justina sat up in the bed. "Where are you going?"

He looked at her over his shoulder. "I have a plan."

CHAPTER 17

The large wooden doors of Castle Acquitaine groaned open.

Laszlo reined his horse tightly, even though the steed beneath him sensed his anger and hatred. As leader now, he would never leave. His brother had been killed in the night by a coward, an assassin. He wanted revenge. He wanted to slaughter every last person in Acquitaine, especially their leader, Damien. After they had butchered the Lady of Acquitaine, the Lord had retreated into the castle, behind the safety of the closed doors for days now. Finally, finally, someone would come forth to be killed.

His men were nervous behind him, but they would not defy his orders. Half wanted to return home. Half wanted the same revenge he wanted. He had to prove himself, as well as seek vengeance for his brother.

A man on a black horse rode forward, followed by an army of men. The man wore black armor and on his tunic was the white dove heraldry for Acquitaine.

Laszlo tightened his fist in the reins and his horse danced anxiously. It could only be Lord Damien. It could only be the ruler of Acquitaine. He gritted his teeth. The weak ruler would die this day.

The group of armored knights and footmen stopped across the field. The two sides remained seated, still, summing each other up.

Finally, Damien cantered his horse forward.

Laszlo spurred his horse, moving forward to meet the weak ruler.

Damien stopped his horse before Laszlo.

Laszlo moved his horse from side to side before him, anxious to strike. Anxious for blood to spilled.

"You will not win," Damien promised. "Surrender now and return home."

"There will be no surrender," Laszlo growled. "My brother is dead, killed by one of your cowards. I will take Acquitaine and all inside will be killed."

Damien flipped up the visor of his helmet to stare at Laszlo. The same hate and fury burned in his eyes. "You've been warned." He whipped his horse around and charged toward his army.

Laszlo returned to his men. He sized up the Acquitaine army. They had the same amount of men as him. The two armies were evenly matched. Except his men were feared and trained where the Acquitaine men were weak and soft.

Suddenly, from behind him, his men began to murmur. He swung his head around to look at them, all fine, battle-hardened warriors. One man pointed to the top tower of Acquitaine's castle. The sun rose, directly behind the figure in white.

"An angel," one of his men whispered.

If Laszlo didn't know better, he would have believed

the woman was an angel. Her golden hair waved in the breeze, her white dress flowed around her. Laszlo recognized her, even from this distance. Confusion and disbelief swelled inside of him. "It can't be," he snarled. "It can't be. I killed her! I cut her braid from her head!"

Damien heard him. He turned.

"It's not her!" Laszlo screamed. He turned back to them to see fear in their wide eyes. Some whispered, some prayed. Their horses moved beneath them nervously, pacing. One reared onto its hind legs.

"But you killed her," Kiprian, his first lieutenant, hissed.

Others around him nodded agreement.

Laszlo swung to look again at the woman at the top of the tower. It looked like her. No one could have the same hair, so golden it rivaled the rays of the sun.

"You killed her," someone repeated from behind him.

"We can't win against an angel," another said.

"No!" Laszlo shouted. "It is a trick! That is not Aurora of Acquitaine." He drew his sword and kicked his steed, hard. His horse charged forward.

Damien answered his charge. His horse galloped forward, his sword flashed in the morning sun as he drew it and held it up. Behind him, the Acquitaine men followed, racing into a battle they could not win.

Fury snarled Laszlo's lips. He chanced a glance over his shoulder. Half of his men followed, the other half retreated into the forest. A howl of rage issued from his throat. Even half of his men could slaughter the Acquitaine men. He pointed his sword forward. He would not back down from this fight. They had killed his brother, Hogar. The deed would not go unpunished.

Before he could reach the Lord of Acquitaine, the sound of clanging swords echoed behind him. He swiveled his head. Shock washed over him. Another army, a larger army, appeared from the depths of the forest, descending into the clearing toward his retreating men.

They were trapped, caught between the Acquitaine men and this new army.

Laszlo threw his head back and growled. He would never surrender. He would slice through the men and enter the castle to slaughter everyone. Acquitaine would fall.

Damien came charging toward him.

And their lord would be the first one killed.

Their swords met with a thunderous sound that echoed across the clearing. Laszlo swung again and again, but Damien matched his blows with as much hatred.

"She should be dead," Laszlo growled.

Damien didn't reply. He leapt at him, knocking him from his horse and both tumbled to the ground. Damien landing on top of Laszlo. He elbowed him in the face with his armored limb.

Stunned, Laszlo took a moment to recover.

It was enough. Damien put a dagger to his throat.

The metal was cold against his skin, and as surprising as the fall to the ground. Laszlo grimaced, staring into cold, black eyes. He waited for death. He waited for the end, for the cut across his throat, but the moments stretched on. A slow smile eased across his lips. "Your society is gentle. It has laws. You can't just kill me."

"Sentence for you has already been decided," Damien growled. "I just wanted you to realize you and your army have been defeated. The Hungars will fall under

Acquitaine rule now."

Laszlo's lips thinned with anger. With hatred. "Never," he hissed. He lifted his sword arm.

With a quick swipe of his wrist, Damien ran the blade across Laszlo's throat.

Laszlo gurgled as his lifeblood ran from the cut.

Damien leaned close to him. "I killed your brother."

Rage turned Laszlo's face red and he reached for Damien.

Damien sat back and watched him die.

Gawyn stood at the city gates, watching the battle unfold. A line of five soldiers stood behind him. His orders were not to let any Hungars enter the city. He clenched his sword tightly, wanting desperately to battle at Damien's side. He also knew this was a battle of revenge for Damien. His brother needed to avenge Aurora, to take out his anger over everything these barbarians had done to her. Everything she had endured.

Gawyn clenched his sword. He felt the same need course through his body. A Hungar had taken away Justina's brother. She was hurting because of Adam's death. And Gawyn wanted revenge for that. But his responsibility was to protect the city. No Hungar would pass over the drawbridge.

Gawyn began to pace. The need to be part of this battle coursed through his veins. And yet, he would not abandon his post.

He watched the Acquitaine soldiers battle the savages. He had trained most of these men and he knew they were skilled fighters. And yet, he watched his men struggle against the onslaught of the barbarians. They made mistakes that Gawyn cringed at. He watched the Hungars. The way they fought, looking for an opening, a weakness. "What do you see?" Gawyn asked the five knights behind him.

For a moment, no one said a word.

"Look at the way they fight," he said to them as well as himself.

The Hungars were just a few inches shorter than his men, but they fought relentlessly, hammering down on the Acquitaine soldiers with swords, axes and clubs. It reminded Gawyn of a bear he had once seen in the court of a noble when he worked for Roke. The bear was fighting an armored man, fighting for its life. It attacked on its hind legs, overwhelming the knight, coming down from above.

Even though the knights were just inches taller than the Hungars, the Hungars used their power to reign blows down from above. The knights were hard pressed to defend this kind of overwhelming brute force.

"They leave their middle open," one of the guards said from behind him.

Gawyn nodded. "They attack from above. If you can go to your right and attack their side or back, you would have a chance. You cannot beat them with a head on attack." That was it. That was the defense.

Suddenly, a group of Hungars pushed forward, skirting the soldiers and headed for the castle at a run.

Gawyn looked back at his men. "Don't avoid the battle. Deflect, sidestep and attack."

The men nodded and clutched their weapons in anticipation.

"Don't let them in," Gawyn commanded. "We must hold the city."

As the Hungars charged across the drawbridge, their stomping, heavy feet sounded like thunder on the wooden planks of the bridge.

Gawyn clutched the pommel of the sword in two hands. He was going to be able to exact revenge for Adam and for Justina. He clenched his teeth and stepped forward to greet the first Hungar with a swing of his sword. It connected with his side and Gawyn quickly moved to the side as the Hungar's hammer slammed down to the earth.

He thrust his weapon, slicing into the Hungar's side. The Hungar staggered.

Gawyn whirled just in time to avoid another Hungar's swing. It crossed the air he had just been in.

Gawyn shoved the fatally wounded Hungar forward so he knocked into the Hungar with the sword. But the Hungar with the sword shoved his friend aside and came after Gawyn again, swinging.

Gawyn blocked the blow and it jarred his entire arm. He spun to the side and struck, slicing at the Hungar. Instead of piercing the barbarian, his sword bounced off harmlessly. Armor! He was wearing armor beneath his animal pelts.

The Hungar spun, bringing his blade around. Gawyn barely had a moment to draw back. The tip of the Hungar's blade pinged off Gawyn's chest plate armor. He backed and the Hungar drove forward, swinging his sword down again and again.

Gawyn stepped out of the way and blocked the strikes. Each block felt as though a wall of bricks had fallen on his arm. He was tiring. Every time he tried to put distance between them, the Hungar pursued him, refusing to allow Gawyn a moment to recover or to think.

And then a blow landed against his sword with

enough strength that he fell backward, his sword went flying to the side.

The Hungar approached slowly, a grin on his face.

Gawyn looked around. His weapon lay in the dirt an arm's length to his right. Behind the Hungar, four of his men were battling one last Hungar.

The Hungar with the sword stood over Gawyn, lifting his sword high in the air for the finishing blow. Like a bear, Gawyn's mind repeated. His middle and legs were wide open. Gawyn acted instinctively. He kicked forward, shoving his booted foot hard into the Hungar's right knee.

As the Hungar howled in pain, his knee buckled. The tip of the sword continued to drop, but the angle had changed to Gawyn's left. He rolled out of the way, grabbed his sword and stood, thrusting his blade into the Hungar's side beneath his plate armor.

Stunned, the bear stood still for a moment before he toppled to the side like a felled tree.

Breathing hard, Gawyn looked at his men. The Hungar's were dead around them. Grimes was holding his side as another knight supported him with an arm around his shoulders. Gawyn moved to Grimes.

Grimes nodded. "I'll be fine."

"Get him to the physician," Gawyn ordered. He turned to look out at the battle in the field. Only a few fights remained. Many Hungar's lay dead across the wide field. Amidst the corpses were scattered soldiers from Acquitaine. To the left side of the field, a large group of Hungars stood, surrounded by mounted knights.

Gawyn also saw another army mixed with the Acquitaine men.

Through the carnage and the destruction, Gawyn

sought out his brother.

Damien stood in the middle of the battle, clutching his sword, standing over a Hungar. He glanced around until he locked eyes with Gawyn.

It was over.

Gawyn took a deep breath and nodded his head once. It was over.

Damien returned his acknowledgement.

The city was safe. Gawyn had kept the city from the Hungars.

Anxiety filled Justina. She paced her chambers, waiting for Gawyn to come back. She moved to the window but could not see the fight she knew was taking place. She pounded the ledge in frustration and moved toward the door. She came up short and groaned softly. She had given him her word she wait here for him. She couldn't help this horrible sense of dread that rose inside of her when he wasn't there.

She knew it was irrational, but after Adam's death, she felt...vulnerable and lonely. She hated it. She hated feeling that way. It wasn't who she was, who she wanted to be.

Suddenly, the door opened. Gawyn stood in the doorway, breathing heavily as if he had run the entire way.

Just the sight of him sent relief coursing through her. She almost trembled with it.

His gaze moved over her. "Going somewhere?"

She threw herself into his arms.

He caught her and held her against him.

His embrace was warm and comforting and strong.

She sank into him, his rich male scent, his reassuring touch. He was all she could ever want. He had told her that he loved her. And she realized she loved him, also. Desperately.

He kissed the top of her head, his hand stroking her back. "It's over," he whispered.

She pulled back to look into his brown eyes.

"Aurora's cousin's betrothed aided in the battle. The Hungars were overtaken, either captured or dead."

"It's over?" she repeated in disbelief.

Gawyn nodded.

She should have felt happiness, she should have felt relief, but the sadness lingered. "It doesn't bring Adam back."

Gawyn shook his head. "I'm sorry, Justina. I brought you both here... I never thought –"

She pressed her fingers against his lips, stopping him. "This isn't your fault. How could you have known? How could I have known?" She shook her head. "It just doesn't help the pain." Her eyes watered as she looked up at him. "I miss him."

Gawyn nodded. "Me, too."

Justina looked down at Gawyn's plate armored chest. She ran her hand over its cold hardness. "I have to go home."

Gawyn tightened his grip on her. "This is your home now."

Justina shook her head. "This can never be my home."

"Stay here. I'm sure there's work you can do here. Aurora will find something."

Justina's brows knit. "I can't." She looked up at him. "I can't stay here."

"I want you to."

She placed a hand on his cheek. "I can't. Not here

with your brother. There is no justice for my father."

Agony swept over Gawyn's face. "He's not the same man."

Justina knew part of that savage killer still lived inside of Damien. She had glimpsed it when they returned Aurora to him. She softly shook her head. "He is when I look at him."

Gawyn looked away from Justina toward the stone floor, his brow furrowed with conflict and anguish. His hands slipped from her body. He nodded and stepped away from her.

Cold invaded the space where his body had been. Justina wanted to reach for him. Instead, her fingers curled into fists.

"Where will you go?"

She couldn't look at him, either. It was just too painful. She didn't want to give him up, but she knew this was his home. At the castle. "I want to rebuild. Uncle Bruce would have wanted it."

He turned away from her. "I don't like you being out there alone."

Justina grinned a humorless smile. "I'll be fine."

"I'll make sure you have adequate protection." He nodded to himself. "I'll send supplies with you and people to help you build."

"Gawyn," Justina called. "I can't thank you enough for all you've done for me."

Gawyn stared at her, and his slow gaze moved over her face.

Sadness grew inside of her. She didn't know if she could give him up. She loved him so. He was all she had left. Her family was gone.

She was afraid, she realized. She was afraid of losing him, too. Better this than loving him and having him taken from her.

She turned away, steeling her breaking heart, as he quietly left the room.

Gawyn couldn't make Justina stay. And he couldn't leave. He had abandoned Damien long ago and he had vowed never to leave him again.

He escorted Justina to the clearing before the city wall. Guards waited for her with the wagons of supplies Gawyn had collected near the forest. His hungry eyes swept her, trying to memorize every curve of her small body. He trembled with unease and want. He didn't know what to say to her. With every part of his being, he wanted to go with her. He wanted to be part of her life as her husband.

He would never propose marriage when he knew he could not be with her. He glanced over his shoulder. Damien and Aurora stood in the road. Aurora had insisted on coming to say goodbye to her and Damien would never let her out of his sight again, Gawyn was certain.

Justina turned to them after inspecting the wagons. Her brown and white mare waited near the wagons. She looked at Gawyn for a very long moment, sadness in her large eyes. Then, her gaze shifted to Damien and the sadness vanished to be replaced with unease and fear.

Gawyn knew she was not ready to forgive Damien, if she would ever be. He wished he could make her see that he wasn't that killer anymore. There was nothing he could say or do to make Justina acknowledge that.

Aurora stepped past him to Justina's side. She stared at her for a long, quiet moment before wrapping her arms around her in a tight embrace.

Justina stood stiffly for a moment before melting into Aurora's hug and squeezing her back. The women shared an experience neither would forget.

When they parted, Aurora brushed a strand of hair from Justina's cheek. "You will visit again, won't you?"

Justina grinned. "Of course. Soon."

Everyone knew it was a lie. Gawyn's heart squeezed tight.

Aurora moved to Damien's side.

Justina approached Gawyn, her gaze on the ground. "I can't thank you enough."

"Thank me?" Gawyn echoed. "Don't." He shook his head. "I did nothing."

She placed a hand on his. "You did all you could."

Gawyn stared at her small hand on his. He couldn't stop himself from taking it into his own.

"Come with me," Justina whispered, her voice full and thick.

Gawyn lifted her hand to his lips. "My place is here. In Acquitaine. At Damien's side." He realized how stiff and hurtful his words were and hugged Justina tightly. "I would give it all up for you, Justina. But I can't. I can't leave him. He's my brother."

Justina held him, and a soft, broken sob echoed in his ears. She broke away from his hold and turned quickly, moving to her horse.

Gawyn stood frozen, as if his entire heart had been wrenched from his chest.

"You want to go with her?" Damien asked in

astonishment. His brother stood beside him, staring at him. "Back to her farm?"

"My place is here with you." He looked at his brother. He had left him on that accursed slave ship, abandoned him, and it had taken Damien a lifetime to forgive him. He would never make that mistake again. "I left you once and I won't do it again."

"Good," Damien murmured, unconvincingly.

Gawyn looked back at Justina. He watched her mount her steed and couldn't help the longing and anguish he felt.

Damien stared at the woman. He couldn't even remember her name. He glanced at Gawyn. His brother's eyes were fixed on her as though the sun rose and fell with her. Damien grimaced. What did he see in her? Part of this animosity was jealousy, Damien knew. He had just found Gawyn. He had just gotten his brother back and they had become friends. He depended on him more than he did with anyone else. How dare this woman come between them? He would not give him up.

And then Aurora stepped up beside him, sliding her fingers through his.

Damien looked at her. His entire body ached for longing of her. She was his sunshine, his life. He knew what life was like without her and he never wanted to live that again.

She stared at him with her large, piercing blue eyes filled with sympathy, as though she understood what he was experiencing.

Lord, he loved her. He loved her beyond reason.

Suddenly, Damien snapped his gaze back to Gawyn. Understanding sliced through the jealousy like a sharp blade. Gawyn loved Justina. And it was a moment later that Damien realized he did indeed know her name. Gawyn loved her maybe as much as he loved Aurora.

Damien had been in darkness without her. And he didn't want his brother to be in that world.

Gawyn had saved him over and over again. It was time Damien returned the favor. He released Aurora's hand and turned away from Gawyn as if heading back to the castle. "You're fired."

"What?" Gawyn asked, shocked.

Damien looked at Aurora. "I said…go and be a farmer."

Aurora's lips turned up in proud satisfaction. She had known!

Gawyn stood, dumbfounded.

Damien knew he was doing the right thing, no matter how much he would miss his brother, no matter how much his heart hurt.

"No," Gawyn said. "I'm not leaving you."

Damien turned to him again. "It's not another country. It's on the border of Acquitaine."

Gawyn still shook his head, refusing. "I made that mistake before and I will not do it again."

Damien knew how much Gawyn regretted leaving him on the slave ship when they were young. It all seemed a different time, a different life. He put a hand on his brother's shoulder. "I want you to be happy."

Gawyn's brow furrowed in indecision and confusion.

Damien squeezed his shoulder. "I'll send word if I

need you. I expect you to do the same."

Gawyn's intense gaze, a gaze filled with hesitancy and plagued with an internal struggle, focused on Damien.

Damien felt Gawyn's loyalty to his core, yet he felt his brother's desire to be with the woman he loved. The two brothers stared at each for a long moment before Gawyn grasped Damien and pulled him into a tight embrace.

Damien knew he was leaving. Missing Gawyn had already claimed a dark corner in his soul. Blood bound them, determination brought them together, and loyalty united them.

Gawyn pulled back and looked Damien in the eye. A silent vow of brotherly love passed between them before Gawyn turned and raced after Justina.

He caught up with her, grabbing her hand and spinning her around. He pulled her to him, kissing her tenderly.

Aurora joined Damien, watching Gawyn. "I'll miss him."

Damien nodded in agreement. He wrapped a hand around Aurora's waist and pulled her to his side. Her warmth banished the darkness inside him.

"Will you be all right?"

Damien stared at Gawyn as he walked hand in hand with Justina toward the horse. He grinned. "I'd pay to see him working in the fields."

Aurora smiled. "She'll teach him. He'll be a grand farmer."

"A farmer with a sword."

"At least he will protect our border."

Damien turned to her in surprise. "Always thinking about yourself," he teased, because that was always the last thing Aurora did.

She entwined her hands around his neck. "You said I should start."

"And so you should." He kissed her lips, tasting her, loving her. He would be forever grateful to Gawyn for bringing her back to him.

As Damien and Aurora headed back to the castle, Damien turned one last time to watch his brother depart.

EPILOGUE

Gawyn was breathing hard as he looked up from chopping the wood. Most of the wood they collected had fallen in the forest and they had dragged it back to the farm. He wiped the sweat from his brow with the back of his arm and looked up toward the forest where Justina was gathering bracken for the oxen beds. He scanned the edge of the forest but saw no sign of her.

A tremor of unease coursed through him and he called, "Justina!"

When no response came, he dropped the axe, moving quickly toward the forest.

His heart skipped a beat when he reached the edge of the forest. He scanned the area for her, his instincts taking over. He had to tell himself she was in no danger, to calm himself. He knew brigands and robbers lurked in the woods near Acquitaine. Had one of them found their way to the farm? After the Hungar attack, it was difficult for him to be calm about her safety. When he didn't find her, he glanced at the forest floor, searching. It was only a moment before he discovered a group of crushed leaves. Footsteps. She must have been working here. He scanned the area until he found another crushed batch of leaves and brush.

He saw the path then. It led into the forest. He carefully followed it deeper into the woods until the path disappeared. He froze, listening. No animal sounds. No birds call, no crickets, no noise.

That was when he understood. He grinned darkly. It was all part of the game, part of the training. He had been trying to elaborate on her father's teachings. It never hurt for her to be able to defend herself. He slowly turned to find Justina standing behind him, a dagger held to his throat.

"You make it too easy," she said softly.

"You kicked the brush to hide your tracks this time." Gawyn was proud of her for thinking of that.

Justina smiled.

Gawyn's heart answered, missing a beat. He adored her. "Your feet are planted. It makes it easier to do this." He blocked the hand with the dagger, grabbed her around the waist and pulled her to him in one, quick move.

Her breath escaped in a rush.

He stared down at her through lidded eyes. She was beautiful. Those large brown eyes, her windblown hair. He lifted a hand to tuck a lock behind her ear.

Her chin came up. "Maybe I wanted you to do that."

Gawyn chuckled deeply. "I'm sure you did." Her father taught basic skills on defense and survival, but Gawyn wanted to teach her everything he knew to keep her safe. "You must always keep your knees bent, your feet ready to move. You could have easily avoided my grab."

She wrapped her arms behind his neck. "Then I would have to do the chores."

Gawyn loved the way her lips moved, the feel of her

body pressed close to his. "What else did you have in mind?"

She took his hand and began to lead him back to the cruck with a sly, sultry look on her face, a sexy tempting slant to her eyes.

Gawyn followed her lead with exuberance and excitement. He never knew farming could be so thrilling.

Suddenly, she stopped and turned to him. The look had vanished and there was sincerity in her lovely eyes. She put a hand on his chest. "Are you happy?"

"I will be in a moment." His manhood hardened at the thought of being with her.

"No. I mean are you happy, here with me, on this farm?"

Gawyn scowled, confused at her question.

"You've given up so much. How could this compare with Captain of the Guard?"

Gawyn understood. But she was thinking of this all wrong. It was she that had given up everything. Her Uncle. Her brother. Her father. He cupped her face, gazing at her with anguished longing. He had given up far less than she. "I would be happy anywhere with you."

She sighed against him.

He brushed his lips against her warm, soft ones.

She tilted her head back. "What if I was a gong farmer?"

Gawyn's lips quirked in humor. "I would stand knee deep in shit to be beside you."

Justina traced the v in his shirt. "What if it was thigh high?"

"Then I wouldn't be able to walk." He put his hands about her waist to draw her up against him. "But I would stand beside you."

"You'd be smelly."

"As would you."

Still, she didn't look appeased; a frown etched into her lovely brow grew deeper.

"Justina," he whispered. "I would go anywhere to be with you, don't you know that?"

She looked down, a frown on her brow. "Why? This life is nowhere near as exciting as your life was. Why would you want to stay here?"

He placed a finger beneath her chin and gently lifted it so her gaze met his. "Don't you know?"

She shook her head. "Know what?"

"You're going to make me say it?" He sighed. "Yes. My life was exciting, and I lived in a grand castle and ate elaborate meals. But my heart was empty. I was lonely."

"Your brother –"

"Is not the woman I love. You are much better to look at than Damien. Your eyes are beguiling." He pressed a kiss to each of them. "Your hair is glorious." He ran an adoring hand down the length of her locks. "Your lips tempting." He lightly brushed his lips over hers. "You are lovely and exciting and…unexpected." He pressed his lips to hers in a long, slow taste of her. "Can't you see how much you mean to me? Can't you see that I love you?"

"You love me?" she echoed, hopefully.

His lips quirked slightly. "I was waiting until you were more comfortable with my past, but I fully intend for you to become my wife."

"Your wife?" she asked, her eyes wide and twinkling.

He scowled. "Of course." He brushed a lock of her hair from her cheek. "But I mean it. I want you to understand who I was and what I have done."

She lifted her chin. "It doesn't matter. Your past means nothing to me. Only the present and the future."

"But you can't forgive Damien. How can you forgive me?"

"You didn't murder my father. And I don't love him."

Gawyn stared at her. He longed for her acceptance and her love. He ached for all of her. "I don't want you to ever regret the decision to be with me."

She stroked his cheek. "I love you and if you love me, there is nothing else to ask for."

Slowly, Gawyn grinned. She was amazing. And beautiful and intelligent. His heart filled with joy. "Then we'd best hurry to the cruck before I toss you to the ground and have you right here."

She giggled and turned, rushing through the tall grasses toward the cruck.

Gawyn watched her for a moment, happiness cresting inside of him. She admitted she loved him. She would be his wife. He started after her, slowly at first, but then he was running.

It was all he had ever dreamed of.

AUTHOR'S NOTE

Thank you for reading Gawyn and Justina's story, Beloved in His Eyes! I hope you enjoyed their happily ever after. If you have a moment and would like to, please leave a review.

Made in the USA
Las Vegas, NV
01 March 2022

44835189R00111